Rosie threw the wire over the man's head and pulled back, jerking the garrote toward him. The wire cut through the vulnerable flesh of the throat, stopping only when it reached the man's neckbone. When Rosie threw the man to the ground, the head rolled backward, like a broken doll's.

Then he took his assault rope from around his chest and unraveled it. Using the hook on one end as a weight, he sent it flying through the air. The hook caught on the top of the high wall the first time. He tugged to make sure it was secure.

Don't worry, Beak, old pal, Rosie thought, using the rope for purchase as he walked up the sheer side of the wall. *This isn't the day you meet your maker.*

THE AKBAR CONTRACT

BOOKS BY MICHAEL MCDOWELL AND JOHN PRESTON

THE BLACK BERETS

THE AKBAR CONTRACT

MICHAEL MCDOWELL & JOHN PRESTON

BLACK STONE PUBLISHING

ISBN 979-8-200-88216-8
Fiction / War & Military

Version 1

Blackstone Publishing
31 Mistletoe Rd.
Ashland, OR 97520

www.BlackstonePublishing.com

To the Rice sisters:
Real women who understand real men

1

Not everyone would understand that this was a vacation. But as far as Sherwood Hatcher, Jr., was concerned, this diversion was as pleasant as a trip to the beach at Galveston.

He would've been surprised if he'd been called by his real name, though. Being called that always threw him. He'd been Cowboy for so many years that he often had to look in his wallet to read the legal handle off his driver's license when he needed to sign a check.

That was just one of the ways life went.

He watched the Pakistanis loading up the C-130. The heat was devastating, but Cowboy didn't mind. Vacations usually involved hot weather, didn't they? Didn't you always go to some-place where you had to strip down to your shorts and had an ironclad excuse to drink margaritas? Sure you did.

The sun was bright here, not far from the desert. Cowboy had on sunglasses, an automatic part of his dress. He sometimes went to bed with them on; to live without the filter of their muted lenses would be utterly alien to him.

Just a little vacation in the Punjab . . .

"Mr. Cowboy"—Karmal came running up to him—"the plane—it's nearly ready for us."

Cowboy looked over and saw that the last of the boxes were being loaded onto the cargo craft.

"Okay, good buddy. Let's get going."

The Afghan warlord had been tagging along ever since Cowboy'd arrived in Pakistan three days before. He'd been Cowboy's constant companion. Since this was a vacation, Cowboy tried to picture the mujahideen merchant as a beach boy. Just make believe Karmal was a beach boy running up to the poolside bar to get you your tequila, and you had the perfect image of recreation and relaxation.

'Course, Cowboy had to acknowledge, it appeared that Karmal was better at getting hold of Ziquriats than cocktails. Those Chinese machine guns, officially called ZPU-1s, were the favorite of the Afghan freedom fighters. Karmal had also been pretty good at getting hold of him. Cowboy had dealt with plenty of sharp numbers in his day, but the deal that Karmal had arranged was the result of some pretty heavy bargaining.

Karmal had made the American pilot think that ferrying this load of munitions to Afghanistan was an act of untold patriotism. He almost had Cowboy convinced that he should have paid for the privilege of taking the cargo across the border into the war zone rather than receive a salary. Almost, but not quite.

Cowboy, like other good soldiers of fortune, believed that ignorance was bliss. He didn't have a single clue as to where the mujahideen got the Chinese weapons, and he wasn't about to ask.

All he knew was that the C-130 was full of them and of the 12.7-millimeter rounds that made them go bang. And he knew that there were a whole lot of people over in Afghanistan who wanted to get their hands on all of it.

Cowboy and Karmal finally got into the plane and walked up to the cockpit. Cowboy sat down at the pilot's controls. He felt right at home, just as if he were sitting down to a meal of chicken-fried steak in Oklahoma.

Cowboy had learned to fly when he was a child. His daddy had been a barnstormer, going from town to town in Texas and the rest of the Southwest, doing anything that had to do with planes that would feed his family.

Daddy'd been in air circuses; he'd flown crop dusters; he'd been in the old-fashioned airplane races; and he'd even, when times were really hard, taken jobs working as a pilot for some of the small airline companies that were coming up.

Hatcher Senior had begun to teach his baby boy almost as soon as the tyke'd been born. Cowboy wasn't sure, but he thought he might have made his entrance into the world during a flight from Houston to Midland when his momma had been copiloting; the family folklore wasn't authoritative about this point.

For many years, the Hatcher family had blissfully ignored the laws about flying licenses and had logged in supervision and the rest of the bull that you had to go through to legally take an airplane into the sky. Cowboy could fly—they could all see that. There was no need for the red tape.

Cowboy'd been perfectly happy to go along with it until one day he realized that there were jet planes that could go faster and climb higher than anything he'd ever gotten his hands on.

He *had* to be able to fly those birds! He just had to. It was then that ugly reality moved into his life. People explained to him that you had to go to college to get behind the controls of those things. Worse, the next generation of them was going to be powered by those strange computer do-hickeys.

Cowboy, who'd barely seen the inside of a classroom before

the day he was told about the jet planes of the future and the computers that were going to run them, turned over a new leaf. You had to go to college? Then Cowboy went. You had to have good grades to get in? Cowboy became a star pupil. He walked through the gates of Texas A&M University the first day they'd let him, and he put his nose to the grindstone for four years, the longest period of self-discipline—maybe the only one—he had endured in his lifetime.

There had been girls who loved A&M men. Cowboy never met them. There had been whores who lived off A&M men and made themselves famous when their exploits moved to Broadway in the hit play *Best Little Whorehouse in Texas*. Cowboy had never spent his money at the Chicken Ranch. There had been football games there, too, and Cowboy had kept hearing about something called the Cotton Bowl up in Dallas that many of his classmates were always wanting to go to. Cowboy never went.

For those four years, Cowboy had submerged himself into the strange identity Sherwood Hatcher, Jr. He'd walked out of College Station with his degree, an invitation to fly jet planes for Uncle Sam in Vietnam, and a whole lot of catching up to do.

The piece of paper that said he'd graduated never meant a thing to him, and he couldn't even remember where he'd put it. But he'd flown a hell of a lot of planes since then. And he'd had a hell of a lot of sex.

That's why taking this bird over the mountains of Afghanistan seemed like a vacation.

Well, those were some of the reasons.

Cowboy got a hand signal from some of the ground crew. He jerked his thumb into the air to acknowledge, and then he began the process of turning on the C-130's engines. The metal frame of the craft shook with vibrations as they came to life, one by one.

Yes, sir, starting up a good old American plane on a little run for the money was his idea of a good time. He should be used to it. There was, after all, that time in Nam.

Cowboy shook his head slowly when he thought of it. Not for the usual reasons Viet vets respond that way to their memories. Sure, Cowboy had all the regular memories of the place—he wouldn't deny that. But he had some special ones as well—the ones that had to do with his becoming the man he was today. That had something to do with this vacation, too.

This was his first solo job in years. No one knew where he was. No one knew what he was doing. He'd told them he needed some time off and that this was how he'd decided to take it—that was all. He needed to get away from them.

But he was going too fast—he was skipping over how *they* had become *them*. That was the Nam stuff. That was what'd made him shake his head. *They* were the Black Berets. During the war, the CIA and some of the other honchos in Saigon and Washington had decided that they needed one force that could move through the Southeast Asian jungles and accomplish things that no one else could even be trusted to know about, let alone trusted to accomplish.

They'd found this half-breed Cherokee named Billy Leaps Beeker, the kind of Marine who makes you think his blood runs camouflage instead of red sometimes, and they'd told him to go out and find a team. Take the best, they'd told him; forget the artificial separation of the different services. Find who you need, and his ass is yours.

Cowboy's behind had been one of the first that Beak had grabbed. So long Air Cavalry, hello Black Berets. Then Beeker had gone and found the rest of them. There'd been a big black buck of an Army Ranger named Roosevelt Boone who'd saved Beak's life at DaNang. He got signed up. Then there were these two strange—really weird—Navy SEALs that Beeker had dragged out of some bar in Hue. He put their names on the dotted line as well.

Actually, it took two lines for one of the swabbies to sign up: Haralambos Georgeos Pappathanassiou by name. Thank God you could get by just calling him Harry. But it'd be just as well if you lived out your life without calling his sidekick anything. Marty Appelbaum was the single most warped human being that Cowboy'd ever known, and that was saying something.

And that was them—the Black Berets. They'd pulled some stunts in Nam. They truly had. There were things that they'd done—things that'd had to be done—that no Senate committee and no *Washington Post* reporter had ever discovered. They never would, either.

There'd been good times, strange times. There'd been all the hard times of war—the times that take flyboys from Texas A&M and turn them into men, Cowboy figured.

Karmal nudged Cowboy's elbow. The mujahideen leader was anxious. It was time to take off. Cowboy shook his head, angry with himself. The problem with settling for doing a job cheaply was that the boss always thought you were less competent. He was letting Karmal have this little errand for almost nothing, and now the man was going to lord it over him.

Cowboy nodded; he'd get the thing going. He revved up the engines and began to move the bird to the end of the runway. He turned around and looked over the landscape to see if he was clear for takeoff. This was supposed to be a clandestine operation. That meant, Cowboy figured, that only a hundred bureaucrats in Islamabad and Washington and a dozen in Kabul and Beijing—along with a handful in London, Teheran, Moscow, and Delhi—knew about it. In any event, there was no control tower here.

He let the throttle out, and he and Karmal were on their way down the runway.

The plane rushed down the strip. It moved faster and faster. It began to lift off; the straight line of its flight turned into an arc. Then there was that moment of ecstasy when the plane lifted off the land, that moment of freedom. And then—ah! Yeah! The plane was in the air, and Cowboy was in control. *Feel that!* Just feel that, he thought to himself as he pulled back on the controls and let himself glide up into the sky.

Now, this was time off!

Damn, wouldn't Appelbaum be pissed if he knew?

Cowboy laughed as he pictured the short blond squirt dancing around screaming and yelling because once again they'd cut him out of the action.

Thing was, Nam hadn't been the end of the Black Berets. Marty Appelbaum was still a part of Cowboy's life. They'd tried to separate when the war was over. They'd all gone back to the States, and they'd tried to become civilians. That had worked for a whole lot of guys, but not for them.

Why? That was one question they never stopped asking themselves. What was there about them that had made it impossible for them to exist in the real world? Had something happened to them that was really that different from what'd come down on all the rest of the guys in Nam? There were times when they'd be honest enough to admit that they didn't really want to know the answer. At those times they just wanted to go on with life.

Knowing might, for one thing, tell Cowboy too much about why he was running this trip into Afghanistan. He knew that Appelbaum would have gone on a patriotic binge and bragged that it was for the sake of the war against communism. If Cowboy'd believed that, he would've taken the whole contract that

Karmal had tried to push on him. But he'd refused; he only wanted the one flight. He wanted one trip over the mountains into Afghanistan. Was it for the sake of anticommunism?

That didn't cut it with Cowboy. But then, why was he willing to take time away from the team to pull a stunt like this? Did he want it as a bragging trophy, to be able to say that he'd been in still another war? Was it the danger? The intrigue? Anger at the idea that you can't be a regular guy and take some time off, 'cause if you did, you'd lose it all—whatever *it* was?

He'd gone back to civilian flying after Nam. That was the obvious choice for him. He'd gone back home to Texas, and for a while he'd worked for some commuter lines. Then he'd met some very interesting gentlemen who had some very small cargoes that just had to be brought over the Caribbean Sea into the United States. If Cowboy would take one of their private planes—Learjets often; sometimes birds that weren't as exotic—and make the hop between Baranquilla and New Orleans, say, or perhaps Bogotá and Miami, they'd pay Cowboy a great deal of money, they said.

They also wouldn't be very upset if Cowboy sampled their wares. After all, what was a little bit of white powder when it went to their favorite, most trustworthy pilot, when he was being so very accommodating and making it unnecessary for them to bother with the customs officials in either Colombia or the States?

That's when Cowboy began to think of jaunts like this as moments of relaxation. Because after Nam they were. They sure as hell were compared to what came after that one episode in Cowboy's life.

It seemed that those damned bureaucrats in Washington had been spoiled by some of the toys they'd gotten used to in Nam, toys like the Black Berets. They'd gone to Beaker, the half-breed leader who was wasting away teaching phys ed to a bunch of snot-nosed brats in some private school near his home in Shreveport, and they'd told him to get the team back together again.

On the surface, Cowboy shouldn't have been interested. He hadn't needed the money, and he had had no desire at all to go back to the military life. Cowboy had been living in a high-rise in Houston back then. He had still been making up for the deprivation of his college days by spending as much time with the ladies of the world as he could.

But surface impressions or no, when Beeker had come and told Cowboy that they were going back, Cowboy had gone with him.

The rest of them had, too. Cowboy had been the one to fly the plane around the country to gather them up together. They'd found Harry running a bar on the South Side of Chicago, a workingman's saloon, the kind that served you a shot and a beer when you got off work. They walked into the place, saw the living death that Harry was surviving, and they'd offered him his salvation: *We're going back.*

Back to where? That was one of the strangest parts of it all, because Beeker had never said they were going back to a place. That wasn't it. And they weren't really trying to go back to Vietnam, although their first group action had led them there. Instead, they were going back to a state of being. They were going back to being Black Berets and whatever the hell that meant. Harry hadn't hesitated even as long as Cowboy had. He'd thrown down his apron and tossed out the few patrons that were left, and they'd gone.

Rosie'd been next. The black man had gone home to Newark. Rosie was one of those men who wasn't . . . well, Rosie was different. Maybe it was stuff that'd happened in Nam. Maybe it was growing up on the streets of one of the most desperate ghettos in America. Who knows? You don't waste many *maybes* on a man like that.

They'd found Rosie peeling the skin off cadavers in the basement of Newark General Hospital. There weren't many people who'd do that for a living. But it had to be done. Skin is the best bandage in the world for severe burn victims. Rosie being who he was, well, Rosie could stand there in the basement and sing lullabies to the dead people while he worked on them, telling them sweet nothings about the pretty babies they were going to save with their sacrifices.

Rosie'd come with them. They were together again.

Well, together with Appelbaum. That nerd was the one thorn in the butt for all the Berets. The problem was, he knew bombs. But Marty didn't just know *about* bombs; he had become *one* with bombs. Appelbaum, who had to be the most annoying, most difficult, most obnoxious human being in the world, was also the world's best demolition expert.

They'd tried to do without him, but he'd ended up back on the team somehow. He'd been earning a good living doing what he did best: blowing things up. Marty'd become a pro at demolition. His speciality had been implosions, the use of explosives to make structures, usually in inner cities, fall in on themselves, not outward, where they'd damage anything close to them.

With skills like those, he was back on the list with the rest of them.

"Mr. Cowboy!" Karmal was tugging at the flier's sleeve, forcing him back into the present. They'd long ago crossed the border. "Mr. Cowboy! The mountain!" The haughty demeanor of the eagle-beaked Afghan leader was gone. He looked scared now. Cowboy liked this change of attitude. So much for the bullying he'd taken and the haggling over prices.

"Piece of cake, good buddy," Cowboy answered. The slope

was coming awfully close. Cowboy had to admit that they did make their mountains big around this part of Afghanistan. But he'd seen the peak as they'd approached it and had automatically understood what had to be done.

He banked the plane sharply so that it traveled parallel to the ridge. Then he flew back and forth, letting the craft climb as quickly as it could. After a few minutes of the maneuver, they were able to climb over the very top of the barrier and cross over it.

"*Aaaaiiiieeee!*" Karmal was screaming, ferociously praying. At least, Allah's name was being repeated a whole lot of times. 'Course, Cowboy realized, it could've been that the man was swearing a blue streak just as easily.

"What is your problem, boy?"

But Karmal had bolted for the back of the plane, holding his hand over his mouth. Cowboy couldn't understand it. There had been *at least* six inches between the belly of the plane and the mountaintop. There was no reason for the guy to go bonkers about it. It wasn't a close call, not really. The guy must just be airsick, Cowboy decided.

The plains that led to Kandahar were in front of them now. The airstrip wasn't too far away. This was the section of Afghanistan where the Afghan freedom fighters were most powerful. They had no air power, though—that was the problem. Even here, the Russkies could come flying down with one of the MiGs they used here, or even with a Hind gunship. Then the C-130, a defenseless transport, wouldn't have much chance of survival.

But what the hell? A vacation had to have some excitement. Cowboy could've slept on the beaches of Rio if he'd wanted to be bored.

And for a member of the Black Berets, this wasn't real excitement in any event. That was the thing of it—that this was what he'd consider time off.

The point was, the Black Berets had spent the last years as a team not just as a lark, but as a vocation. They'd put themselves out for hire to the biggest bucks and the most pressing causes in the world. Their itinerary had spanned the globe.

When he'd been flying cocaine, Cowboy had gotten to love the drug. He'd loved it so much, there'd been nights when his nostrils bled—and he hadn't cared. There'd been nights when his reality was constructed out of chemicals—and he had not known it. There'd been nights when he'd seen God—and he had not remembered.

But being a Black Beret, he'd come to realize, was something just as addictive and just as dangerous as cocaine or any other drug he'd ever taken. It was something you couldn't shake, cold turkey or any other way. Being a Black Beret meant you'd sold your soul to Billy Leaps Beeker and that he had it in his hand for the rest of your life. 'Cause once you were a Black Beret, you couldn't live without it.

Karmal had finally come back into the cockpit and taken his seat. It was bad timing on his part, Cowboy realized, because now the mujahideen was going to have to get ready for the other half; the inevitable result of any roller-coaster ride up, was one—

"*Aaaaiiiieeee!*" There went Allah again.

The bitch of it was, Karmal couldn't get up this time because of the sharp angle of descent the plane was in; he was forced to stay seated. Cowboy took off his Stetson—regretting it terribly since he'd just bought it in Houston on the way over here—and handed it over. It'd have to do for a bag on this trip. There weren't any pretty stewardesses to hand out disposable ones.

No hassle; Cowboy had a few more. And he knew he could buy the damned factory if he wanted to. That was another thing about the Berets.

It seemed that every time they went out on a mission, they

came back with more money. He knew all about that since he was the official banker of the group. The rest of the bozos didn't care; and even if they did, they wouldn't have known how to juggle a checkbook, let alone the eight-figure Swiss bank accounts and investment trusts that Cowboy had finagled for them.

That was still another problem, because it took so much pleasure out of life. Another man in Cowboy's position would have been happy to go to Las Vegas and spend his vacation rolling some dice, playing some blackjack, getting a kick out of risking the kid's college tuition and thinking he was living dangerously.

But Cowboy could squander a couple million, and it would hardly eat into the interest payments coming from their investments.

Money had lost its meaning for the Berets. Not that they'd ever really wanted a whole lot. The only one who really spent any was Beeker, and that was to continue his relentless purchase of land near their home base, a sprawling property centered near Shreveport, Louisiana. Sometimes it seemed as if the half-breed were trying to buy back America for his people. They had holdings now in Louisiana, Arkansas, Texas, and Oklahoma, and the damned man was still buying.

Cowboy sniffed the foul smell coming from Karmal in the next seat. The plane was leveling off now; the man got up and ran back to the john as soon as he realized that the level of descent was even enough.

Well, that was the way it went when you were on vacation sometimes. Someone was always doing stuff like that.

It was actually a beautiful day for flying, Cowboy realized. Too bad the kid wasn't there. Even in the middle of this little jaunt into Afghanistan, Cowboy couldn't help but smile when he thought about Tsali. Damned good kid. No problem there.

The rest of them may be the strangest set of individuals he'd ever met, but no one could say a thing bad about Tsali and mean it.

He was a full-blooded Cherokee. That was something hard to find these days. It had appealed to Billy Leaps, feeding on the man's mystical belief in his own people and heritage. Beeker had found Tsali one day a few years back when he'd been out hunting. He'd only meant to find himself some woodchuck, but he'd come across these rednecks in the forest tormenting this teenage Indian boy.

Too bad for them. Beeker could be a mean bastard when riled. He got his dander up that day—enough that the pair of them had ended up six feet under in the Louisiana dirt. The kid had ended up living with Beeker in what was, back then, just a shack in the woods. And more—the kid had become one of them. None of them minded that he was a deaf-mute. None of them thought that meant he was less of a person, that his humanity was handicapped.

Tsali was one of Cowboy's favorite people in the world. Maybe his number one. The kid'd grown up with them, had lost his cherry on a visit to a cathouse with Cowboy—that was the kind of thing that made you close to a youngster, being the one that took him to get laid for the first time.

But he was more, in many ways. He was really the reason Beeker was buying all that land. He was, in the end, the only reason the rest of them had for continuing to build up huge cash deposits long after they'd accumulated more than they'd ever spend themselves. The idea of Tsali going without in this life was something they couldn't stand to contemplate. Send themselves all back to the Stone Age, and they probably wouldn't mind. But they'd do anything for the kid, each one of them.

Cowboy scowled. Tsali was all well and good, and maybe he was the one thing that gave their life together on the Shreveport farm a semblance of humanity. But it didn't change one thing: that their lives as Black Berets were warped. Totally warped. *Look at me*, he thought to himself. *I'm turning out as bad as Appelbaum. I think running guns to the Afghan freedom fighters is a damned picnic. This is my frigging vacation!*

"There! Mr. Cowboy! There's the landing strip where my men wait."

Cowboy was wrenched back into the present by the frantic waving and pointing that Karmal was doing now. There was a tone in the man's voice that was more than just a little bit relieved. He wasn't just happy to be getting home, and he wasn't just pleased they hadn't met up with any Russkies. Cowboy did believe the ungrateful son of a bitch hadn't had a good flight.

To hell with it! Cowboy thought. Disgusted with himself and Karmal both, he decided to get the damned bird onto the ground as fast as he could.

"*Aaaaiiiieeee!*"

"Well, damn it, Karmal! You hurt my feelings!" Cowboy yelled as he aimed the plane for the ground, nose first.

But Cowboy knew what he was doing. He pulled out at just the moment when the craft was at the edge of its tolerance and leveled her off. Then, remarkably, the landing gear was down, just in time. And equally wondrous, he laid the tires onto the rough strip with all the care and nurture of a mother putting her baby into the crib.

The engines began to soften as soon as the forward movement of the plane was braked, and Cowboy easily taxied the C-130 over to where the band of mujahideen were waiting for them.

Just in time, too. The smell in the cockpit was getting pretty disgusting.

"Damn, Karmal. You shoulda trusted me more."

2

The temperature wasn't as bad up here in the Afghan mountains as it was back in Pakistan. There the heat had been damned oppressive, even for a southern boy like Cowboy. But there was at least a hint of cool air here. He could relax a bit. Enjoy his vacation.

Karmal had gone away. As soon as the man had got his feet on the ground, all of his overbearing personality had returned to the fore. He was obviously not only the purchasing agent for this outfit; he was its leader as well. He'd pointedly ignored Cowboy after they'd disembarked from the plane. Generals never like to look subordinates in the eye after the underlings have seen them frightened and weak.

Too bad. Karmal may not have been great company, but he was the only one of the group who had any grasp of English at all. But Cowboy'd been able to do his business with some of the others using the universal hand language of soldiers. That was something he'd become especially good at after having learned the sign language in order to communicate with Tsali.

That came in handy with a pair of bright-eyed kids who were hanging around the landing strip. They couldn't have been more than fifteen. It was hard to tell with the children of war. They'd usually grown up with insufficient diets that often stunted their growth.

It never ceased to amaze Cowboy how kids remained kids, though, no matter what. Here they were, in a country desperately fighting a war against all odds, and they had about them all the mischievousness of spoiled brats in the suburbs. He'd seen lots of their kind in Nam and later in other countries around the world. Some of the kids in every war zone were like this.

They slyly walked around him, taking his measure. They were fascinated by the plane. They only played at helping the older men carry off the cargo. They scampered up the superstructure of the aircraft as soon as the elders were distracted. They wanted to see how the propellers worked. They kept trying to ask Cowboy questions, but he couldn't understand their words. The frustration among the three of them was mutual.

He finally just let them go on with their explorations alone. They might pick something up. He wondered what it must be like for them. These people had lived in incredible ignorance and poverty for centuries. They were one of the least literate nations in the world. They had existed as nomadic tribesmen, spending their spare hours fighting with one another over grazing rights. But now they were involved in a major war with a superpower, the Soviet Union.

What went through the minds of these children? Here they were, climbing over the wings of a modern airplane. If it hadn't been for this war, they might never have even conceived of mechanized flight!

Then Cowboy's attention was distracted. The mujahideen were unloading the plane fast now. Awfully fast, it seemed to Cowboy. He watched as they discharged carton after carton of Ziquriats and ammunition off the C-130. Cowboy haphazardly checked the manifest as the pieces were carried away. This was a friendly operation, as above board as arms dealing gets in this day and age. He wasn't worried about any trouble.

There was more on the plane than just the automatic rifles. He wasn't really supposed to know what the cargo was—that was one of the first rules of gun-running. His manifest only showed numbers that corresponded to the markings on the containers. But there was no doubt that some of the larger pieces held the SA-7s that the Afghans loved so much. He wondered how proficient they could be with the hand-held missiles, though. SA-7s were designed to be used by troops in the field, troops who at least had had an American high school education.

These guys who were fighting the Russian invaders were dedicated, and after Nam no American veteran was going to underestimate the abilities of a native force of guerrillas. But still . . .

Man, these guys were in some hurry! They were acting like troops in Nam expecting a visit from Charlie any minute.

Before this brilliant thought could register in Cowboy's mind, there was a too-familiar sound. He felt the blood start to speed up in this body. Then he saw the mujahideen react. That was what they hadn't been able to tell him.

Whoop! Whoop! Whoop!

The sound was still in the distance, but at the rate the new Russian Hinds could move, they were right on their asses. These Afghans were raw. Many of them, Cowboy realized, were just kids no older than Tsali, and many of them were younger than the Cherokee youth's eighteen years. They weren't on the front lines, either; they'd been assigned this supply job. That meant they probably weren't seasoned.

God damn it—what a thing to happen.

Most of the Afghans were making for cover. These guys'd survived by never taking on the superior technical forces that the Russians brought to bear. Instead, they'd used their skills as irregulars, especially the single most important advantage that any occupied people had in war on their home turf: They used the landscape to their own advantage.

The Hind that was coming this way was one of the most state-of-the-art battle helicopters in the world. Cowboy'd flown one on a mission the Berets'd run once. He knew just how good they were and just how deadly their armaments were.

Cowboy wasn't about to spend the rest of his vacation in these mountains. He pushed past the few Afghans who were still near the plane and got to some of the boxes that he hoped really did hold SA-7s.

He grabbed a wrench and pulled open the wooden crates. There the damned things were. Just the way God meant them to be, or at least the way Washington meant them to be. He pulled one out and hefted it up onto his shoulder.

He turned toward the sound. It'd been soft for a while. He had to struggle to locate its source. But it was coming closer now.

The two kids were suddenly standing beside him. Those same two sets of bright eyes were staring at him, intently studying what he was doing.

"Get the hell out of the way, will you, kids? Go on, scoot! Get to the hills!"

They were only teenagers, and this was no time for them to be studying Western technology. They wouldn't budge, though. They seemed to be staring at him. Did these assholes keep mentally retarded kids for pets or something?

But now the *Whoop! Whoop!* was too close for Cowboy to be worrying about babysitting. He turned and saw the Hind come into view. Only seconds remained to deal with this before the Russkies understood that there was something on this landing strip that could fire back at them. Cowboy knew he had to use that advantage if he wanted to get this damned plane—or himself—out of here in one piece.

His mind worked like a computer. He went over the checklist of how the SA-7 worked. It was a heat-seeking surface-to-air missile. If he could fire the damned thing, that Hind was history.

It was a question of resting the missile on his shoulder, sighting the SA-7 this way, then pulling this lever, and . . .

Woooossssh!

The mother took off into the air. The Hind pilot might have had a couple seconds to understand that some prime American technology was coming his way. Cowboy would never know because, long before the Russkie had a chance to fire his own missiles, the SA-7 had found its bull's-eye, and there was a deafening explosion as the helicopter exploded, complete with its own fuel supply and weaponry.

The blast echoed through the mountains. The sounds reverberated over and over again. But Cowboy had already reached for another of the SA-7s and didn't have a chance to enjoy the background music.

He'd become a man possessed. As soon as he'd gotten over the first shock of the danger approaching, he'd realized that the damned Russians were after his plane. If the bastards took away his wings, Cowboy would be taking a long, long walk over those mountains he'd just skimmed. How long would it take him? Two weeks? Three, at least, to get back to the Pakistani border.

There was another Hind now, coming around the same mountain bend as the first one. And this one wasn't going to be surprised.

Cowboy went through his procedure once more. He quickly did his calculations, and he found all the controls he needed. There was that wonderful *Whooosh!* sound and then again, before the copter could fire, the same explosion.

Freedom! What a great feeling! Cowboy stood there with the disposed parts of the missile on the ground and was ready to try to relax. He turned to the two kids who'd stood by him and reached over to ruffle one of their heads.

"Hey, you guys. Put those down. Those aren't toys!" They'd each taken up one of the SA-7s, mimicking Cowboy, evidently. Just like the kids in Nam used to do; they'd wanted to play at being whatever the adults around them were.

But before he could move to take them out of the boys' hands, he heard a new sound. It was like the sound of the approach of the Hinds before, but now it was in stereo.

The *Whoop! Whoop! Whoop!* was echoing this time—or Cowboy thought it was, for one split-second. Then he realized that they were in the real deep kind of shit this time.

He grabbed another missile and stood there and saw that he was gone. He was going to bite it. The mujahideen had run into the hills. Possibly, they could have used those Ziquriats on these copters; the Chinese guns were more than powerful enough to pierce the shells of even the most high-tech Hinds. But there weren't any trained guns around. There was just him and this one damned SA-7. He couldn't possibly get three missiles off in time. At least one of those Hinds was going to be able to answer, and there would go the C-130. And there would go Cowboy.

Well, in good old Black Berets fashion, he'd go down fighting. He took the one missile and went through the steps of preparing to fire it. He felt like Doug Flutie making the Hail Mary pass against Miami, but why not? Hey, everyone's gotta complete a big pass in life at least once.

Just as he pulled the lever that sent the heat-seeking missile flying off toward the lead copter, there was another one of those stereo sound effects.

Those damned kids had fired their own! God damn it!

They'd never been trained on anything like that. They were babies. They were fouling this up. They were—

The three explosions were the most beautiful trio in the history of music, as far as Cowboy was concerned. Beside him, the two boys were jumping up and down and yelling, the way a kid back in the States would yell if his team had just scored the winning touchdown against all odds. Well, wasn't that just what Cowboy'd been thinking?

He turned and watched the pair of them. In his mind they were high schoolers at a pep rally. He put his arms around their scrawny shoulders and hugged them to himself, putting a damper on their enthusiastic display perhaps, but letting them know that he liked their Hail Mary. If they ever wanted to play football, he sure as hell knew some teams that could use their winning attitude.

"It is not good, what they have done." Karmal had recovered his machismo after he'd climbed down from the hills overlooking the airstrip and the littered bodies of the Hinds and their dead crews.

"You mean these kids?" Cowboy yelled at him.

"They misused our weapons. We needed these for a major offensive. They will be punished for this playing."

"This wasn't playing, you no-count goat thief!" Cowboy watched as the two boys were grabbed by some of the adults on Karmal's orders. "Don't you understand? Those kids have been brought up in war, and they've taught themselves by watching adults.

"It's the life you've given them. In the States they'd be studying how some guy drives a car, and then they'd go out on the road and teach themselves. But here they learn how to use simple missiles.

"And by the way, they did it to save your frigging cargo and your plane."

"The plane," Karmal said, waving a hand, "is not ours. It was . . . lent to us by your government."

"Well, it's my way out of this hole. Listen, they saved my life. They saved my bird. They saved your rifles. They should be heroes."

Forcing himself to use a calmer voice, one that wouldn't make the mujahideen leader so defensive, Cowboy went on. "You should reward them for learning so quickly and for reacting so well. You can get more missiles. You know there are more back at the supply depot."

Karmal's eyes narrowed. There came over his face a look that Cowboy recognized all too well, the look of the camel trader, whether dressed in Afghan robes or in the three-piece suit of a Wall Street banker. Cowboy tried to back off a bit. "There are plenty of pilots back there—"

"No. None for many weeks. You were the only one who we could have. They told me this."

"But . . . I'm on vacation."

"The boys will be punished by the old laws." Karmal was faking, just the way any good horse trader would, or so Cowboy tried to make himself believe. "A good whipping—"

"Hold on, José!" Cowboy put up a hand. "You can't—"

"In our country," Karmal continued, "punishment is severe, as is the land. In our country, young men . . ."

Even though Cowboy knew damned well what was happening, he made the mistake of looking over at the kids, who were being held in their elders' arms right now. A look of terror was in their eyes. They weren't going to get a little visit to the principal's office and a few whacks of the ruler out of this one. It was a travesty of justice that they were going to be punished at all.

And Cowboy was more convinced than ever that it was something they were going to suffer not for anything they'd done, but because this bastard wanted a free ferrying job from Pakistan.

"I'll do it." God *damn!* The things he got himself caught up in. A hell of a vacation! Another flight over those mountains with a planeload of contraband. Another chance to run in with a party of Hinds. All of it just to make sure a couple of teenage Afghans didn't get their asses burnt by this fanatic. "But now. Right now. I want to fly back this afternoon. You get the damned plane loaded in Pakistan as soon as you can, and we're back here with the shortest layover possible."

Karmal wasn't so good a trader that he could suppress the smirk of victory that came over his face. He nodded once, curtly. "It will be done."

"And Karmal!" Cowboy called out after the mujahideen leader had turned to get ready. "You bring some paper bags this time, will you? I'm not going to waste another Stetson."

Karmal shot some words to his men, and the boys were released. They'd obviously been told that the American pilot was responsible for their escaping the expected punishment. They came running over to him and grabbed hold of him. He suspected they were saying all the things that he'd heard in country after country from people who he'd helped.

Well, maybe being a nice guy wasn't such a bad thing. And flying a C-130 over a few hills wasn't so bad. He imagined he'd be a hero to these two when they grew up. Maybe they'd want to fly, too.

"What are they saying?" Cowboy finally asked Karmal, who'd come back, evidently ready to reboard the plane, willing to go through the roller coaster once more, all the happier since it was free this time.

Karmal and the boys spoke quickly in a language that

Cowboy couldn't identify. At first the leader seemed puzzled. Then he looked severe. But finally he seemed amused when he turned to Cowboy, and with a voice that carried that unmistakable I-told-you-so tone, he said, "You have spoiled them. They want some present from you. Something I don't understand. But they've heard it on the American short wave."

"Well, what?"

"Something called The Boss. Does this make any sense to you?"

So much for being a hero. But this time Cowboy did reach over and mess up the hair on both kids' heads. The idea that rock 'n' roll could live in the middle of this war gave Cowboy something to be thankful for. Even these kids, schooled in the middle of a foreign invasion, wanted to have their youth.

"Tell 'em they're on. I promise them."

Cowboy stood there for a minute and felt awkward and unsure of himself. "Hell, Karmal, let's get going, will you? I got a vacation to get on with. Let's get this show on the road."

3

Had that little side trip to Afghanistan really been necessary? Cowboy was still pondering what his life had been like for the previous two decades. He'd been just a teenage kid in Texas in the beginning. His momma and his dad may have been a little strange because of the way they earned their living and because of their passion for planes, but it wasn't really that out of the ordinary. There was nothing there that would've told you that this kid of theirs was going to turn into a paid fighter, a mercenary.

Worse, a mercenary whose idea of time off was gun-running in Asia.

The questions plagued him. He had two more weeks before he was supposed to be back in Louisiana. They hadn't been looking for any new assignments, and Beeker had sent them all out, in rotation, to have free time. R&R, just like in Nam—time to make yourself remember you were a human being. Time to go get laid, have a few drinks, see some scenery.

After he made the second delivery to Karmal's mujahideen— with the Springsteen cassette tapes that he'd gotten for a price he didn't even want to think of ever again, except to imagine the grins on those kids' faces—Cowboy'd decided that he had to force himself to do something, well, normal. He wanted to do something that some other Texas A&M grad would do.

That meant beaches, women, and resorts with bars. And in India, that meant Goa. He'd booked himself a flight to the former Portuguese colony and had checked into one of the many hotels that lined its beaches.

The choice was even better than he'd imagined. Since India had forced the Portuguese out of this vestige of its ancient colonial empire, Goa had become the Indian Riviera. Hints of the old colonialism were actually stronger here than they were in the rest of India. The restaurants served a hybrid cuisine that combined European food with the local stuff, with a result not unlike the Cuban variations of Chinese cooking that Cowboy'd had in New York and Miami.

There were also lots of girls in lots of bikinis in Goa. Whole lots of them. And some of them, to his delight, showed off their unmistakable Latin origins.

With a pitcher of margaritas and wearing only his own swimming briefs and omnipresent sunglasses, Cowboy had taken up residence on the terrace of the Nueva Lisboa Hotel. He may have chosen India for his vacation because of its exotic Asian image, but the discovery of an entire province full of beautiful ladies was a little bit of heaven.

This is what a man should do on his vacation, Cowboy told himself, just look at pretty women and get drunk. For two days, Cowboy felt as if he'd accomplished his goal: He'd had no thoughts of flying through flak or that he should be happy living in a house that was really a prettied-up barracks with a group of men. He was on the beach, man, on the beach.

He loved the way the Portuguese-descended ladies looked at him through lowered eyelids and smiled coyly at him, only to break into embarrassed giggles when they caught one another's eyes. Not quite the Latin ladies of his dreams, but close enough.

They did prove occasionally to be a sticky problem, what with all those possessive fathers and brothers bent on protecting the family honor. But he couldn't help himself. He just couldn't resist a beautiful woman, a woman like many of these on the beach.

A trance would eventually come over Cowboy. He would get close to a woman, inevitably bedding her, and then the words would come out of his mouth in all felt sincerity. "Marry me! You have got to marry me!" he'd plead, letting the woman know that his life couldn't go on if she didn't.

Regardless of any family opposition, that desperate appeal was something that few women in the world could resist. Seeing this tall, good-looking, blond flier on his knees, his eyes beseeching her to grant him this one request, was something that most women simply weren't equipped to handle. Many of them— too many of them—eventually caved in.

There would then be the inevitable wedding. The fathers would all be proud; no matter what they'd said earlier, there wasn't a Latin father on earth who wasn't proud on his daughter's wedding day. And the mothers would cry. So would Cowboy, he'd be so happy.

His happiness, and the happiness he gave his wife, would continue well into the honeymoon. Cowboy loved honeymoons. He loved being in love. He adored the blushing manner of his new wife, whichever one she was. And he loved having all their meals brought to their suite—Cowboy loved room service. It was all bliss, just the way the books said it would be.

But then there would also come a moment when the woman would inadvertently begin to nudge her husband toward reality. There would be a conversation about a job or a hint of a new house that needed to be bought, or else there was something about doing a special favor for papa. There would be *something*.

That's when Cowboy would leave. Later, in those very few times when he was caught by one of the women he'd left, he tried to explain that he hadn't stuck around for the formalities of a divorce because that was simply too much for him to deal with. He walked away from all of his marriages with a picture of his perfect bride firmly implanted in his memory.

That was how he always wanted to remember his women: at the church in their white gowns and on their honeymoon night with the enthusiasm that only a bride has.

About halfway through his first day in Goa, as he watched all the people on the beach, he realized what he was really doing; he understood just how seriously he was taking this vacation.

Cowboy was going to get married.

Again.

He even thought he'd found the right lady. Her name was Carmelita, and he'd met her on the beach. She hadn't been dressed quite so brazenly as some of the others. She'd worn a full one-piece bathing suit, not one of those bikinis. But the extra fabric hadn't hidden her physical virtues—far from it.

She'd allowed him to take her to a café for a drink only in the company of a friend of hers. That endeared her all the more to him. After all, he was looking for a wife, not a one-night stand. He wanted to know that the woman was of good virtue.

She was. She'd actually insisted on a second date before she'd gone to bed with him the first time. And what a time it'd been!

Cowboy was waking up in the big double bed of his hotel room, and the memory of her was sending physical pain through his body. Carmelita had been here two nights before. He spread his legs out over the sheet and remembered what it'd been like to have her here next to him.

Her hips had been so firm, and her breasts—he let out a little groan when he thought of them. He ran a tongue over his lips and thought about how those same lips had been caressing her body.

As soon as she returned later today from her family business in a village only a few miles from Panjim, she'd come running into his arms and into his bed once more. He could feel the smooth skin, taste the sweet perspiration, and sense what it'd be like to find himself inside her once more—over and over again.

She was one in a million. In fact, at this very moment Cowboy knew this was the one he should marry. This was the one with whom life would be a perpetual honeymoon.

He staggered to the shower and stood under it for nearly half an hour. He shaved carefully. For once, he paid as much attention to his choice of jockey shorts as he did to his shirt, since he knew the woman would see both. He used his aftershave, the new kind that was so expensive, he wouldn't have bought it if it hadn't been available in the duty-free shop at a fraction of the usual retail cost. And he combed his sparse yellow hair much more painstakingly than usual.

There was a swagger to his walk as he came down the stairs of the Nueva Lisboa and into the lobby. He was practicing the way he'd march down the aisle with her. It would be so wonderful. Such a perfect wedding. First there was the undeniable fact that she was Latin. Added to that was the exotic locale: a marriage in the tropics. The mysterious East would envelop them in its embrace. His mind ran rampant with romanticism.

It was, he realized, a good thing that he was alone on this trip. Beeker and the rest of them had been getting very difficult about weddings. Even Tsali, who never had a negative thing to say to any of the adult men with whom he lived, hadn't taken the last marriage very seriously. But since he was alone, Cowboy could indulge himself and his whims and his need for the image of a life companion—if not the reality.

He sighed contentedly and ordered from the Goan menu. He'd actually missed the real breakfast; this was the lunch hour, and that, he decided, gave him the opportunity to have a bit of champagne. He'd imagine that Carmelita was here with him to drink it.

"Hello, Cowboy."

He froze. He identified her by her odor before he turned and looked at her. There was something about her smell that was unique. They'd talked about it, though never with Beeker, and they'd all agreed about that one fact. There was no question that there was expensive perfume in her smell; this woman was very expensive. But there was always her personal touch as well, something that in any other woman—though never in her—you might think was a little slutty. It was more than sweat, but it was less than saying she was unwashed, because that was certainly not true.

She was a lady, not in the way that Cowboy usually used the term, as embracing all females. But she was a lady in the class way. This was a real, bona fide lady.

He still didn't turn to look at her. He didn't want to. The fact that she was here and that she'd found him meant danger—the real kind, not playacting with the fathers and brothers of jilted brides. When she showed up, trouble was always her companion.

Even when her companion was Billy Leaps Beeker—and that was who Cowboy always saw her with. He wondered now, as he'd wondered many other times, if she cheated on Billy Leaps. He actually assumed that she did. But no, wait—he couldn't say that, could he? As far as he knew, the woman had no agreements with the Black Berets' leader.

Cowboy sensed that the waitress had returned to the table. She must have brought the champagne. He heard the other woman say, "Yes, that's fine. You may pour us two glasses."

How could a man like Billy Leaps—a true warrior, a man awesomely aware of the Cherokee fighting blood in his veins—let a castrating woman like this into his life? Who did she think she was, taking over even the approval of the wine that he'd ordered?

He turned to look at her then. But even with the protection of his sunglasses, it was a mistake. God, she was beautiful! Not just attractive, and not just well dressed and well made up; she was drop-dead beautiful.

Was that why Billy Leaps let her walk in and out of his life so often? Was that why Beeker, of all people, shared a woman with other men?

"You're lookin' good, Delilah."

She smiled, lifted up her glass, and toasted him silently. The edge of the glass went to those perfect red lips, and as she sipped, he could see her teeth; they were so white, he could see the sunlight reflecting off them even through his filtered lenses. He picked up his own glass and tipped it back, drinking the whole of the drink at once. Why not? He had a sinking feeling in his belly that he wasn't going to get married on this trip after all, not now that Delilah was here.

"I know Goa's turned into a *très* chic resort," he said, his words dripping with sarcasm, "but I can't quite believe it's a co-incidence that you showed up here just two days after I arrived."

"Did you enjoy Afghanistan, Cowboy?" she asked, taking another sip of the champagne. He watched her and realized that the wine barely touched those lips of hers, the ones that looked scarlet and always appeared so moist. That was another one of her moves, he figured. She gave you the impression she was drinking with you, but she wasn't really doing anything more than keeping you company—and hoping you'd get drunker than she was and be less able to defend yourself against her mind.

"How did you know?" Cowboy hadn't told anyone, not a soul, even to what continent he was going. He'd just arrived in India ten days before and had found the pickup piloting job while drinking in a hotel bar in Delhi the first night.

"Whenever there's that desperate a cry for a Springsteen recording, we know something's up." She smiled. "It wasn't easy to get, you know. You didn't really think it'd been bought here in India, did you?"

He looked at her quizzically.

"I had it flown in by special courier plane."

"Congress'll love that expense," he sneered.

"Double coverage, Cowboy. The mission's written down as a training flight—no one will question that. It was on a Stealth bomber." Her smile widened. "They don't exist. So Congress can't tell us we can't use them, can they?"

"So you used the most expensive airplane in the world to bring a couple rock 'n' roll tapes to India?"

"I trusted you, Cowboy. There had to be a good reason."

"What do you want, Delilah?"

She looked hurt now, as if he'd accused her of doing something disreputable. "It's not that way, Cowboy. It's just that it's so convenient, your already being here."

"Convenient? Why?"

"Because we need you here. The team."

"Talk to Beeker—he's the head honcho."

"I will. As soon as you tell him to bring the men to India."

"Why me, Delilah? Why not you?"

"Because you're the one with the more pressing reason for them to come."

"How do you figure that?"

He knew he was in trouble when she seemed so serious. She was giving him a look that told you that something was going on in your life and that she cared about it. That was one thing, though: you really thought she did.

But it had to be an act, didn't it? Wasn't everything she did one big manipulation? Or could it be that his feelings and his emotions were important to her? He watched her as she reached for her purse and pulled out a manila envelope. She handed it to him and then lifted up her champagne to drink more—or to appear to drink more.

He knew that whatever was in there was going to be dangerous. Coming from her, it was a Pandora's box. If he were smart, he'd leave it and leave the restaurant. He'd go back to Delhi and get the next flight back to the States.

But he opened it.

There was a series of photographs in the envelope.

Carmelita was unquestionably dead. He felt nausea rise up in his belly when he looked at the images. It wasn't just the idea of death. It was how her corpse was displayed.

She was naked, and she'd been mutilated in a way that no woman should ever even have to think about. The nausea became more powerful.

He put the prints down and poured more wine. He looked at it and then put it down again. Booze wasn't going to help this. His elbows hit the table, and his face collapsed into his palms.

"Did you have anything to do with this?"

"No." She didn't question the fact that he was implying that she might. They both knew that Delilah would go to extremes to get her way, especially when she thought it was the wish of her political masters, whoever they might be.

"Who?"

"Some very dangerous people. Some people who I think the Black Berets had better get to know awfully well.

"There's money in it, Cowboy. A lot of money. But I know

you have a personal interest in the contract now. One that makes your summons to the ranch in Shreveport a lot more compelling than mine."

She stood up. "I have a clear line to Louisiana waiting for you at the consulate. Are you ready to go? The time difference is awkward. But I think they'd take your call. Don't you?"

4

They sat in the penthouse suite of the most luxurious hotel in Delhi.

The blonde woman was the only person here besides the team members. She was also the only one smoking. Her cigarette sent up a thin trail of smoke. They waited for her to say something. They were waiting to hear why they'd been brought halfway around the world—this time; it'd happened before and often.

Delilah worked out of Washington. For that reason and without any other proof, they'd always assumed that she was in the pay of one of the nation's top-secret agencies. And with the press that those outfits had been getting lately, they only hoped that their suspicion was true—that hers was so undercover that it'd never be exposed by a reporter or by some rabid congressional committee.

It might well have been that her employers were private citizens. In fact, more than once they'd even speculated that she might be the employer herself. Why not? They could see that this wasn't some regular honey of a secretary that they were dealing with.

Certainly that's not what Billy Leaps Beeker was dealing with.

The leader of the Black Berets stood up and went to stand by one of the windows. Delhi stretched out below him. He wanted this view because it gave him an excuse not to look at the woman. It was enough to have to smell her; that got to him even worse than it did Cowboy.

If he didn't have to look at her, he might not have to think too much about her. He might be able to regain that professional composure for which he was so well-known. But he also might not break out with the question that was burning inside of him:

Why haven't you called in over three months? Where have you been? Why have you left me alone? And the boy! Maybe you're not his mother, but he loves you as much as . . . Where have you been?

Beeker was a big man, standing over six feet tall, and although he was now forty, he still had all the musculature that he'd developed in his years with the Marine Corps. Even in his civilian clothes—typically, even his civvies were khaki—the physical power of the man was obvious. So was his mobility. It might seem strange to call such a powerful man graceful, but there were few other words that could describe the way he moved. Yet he didn't feel that way now—not with her here in the room. He didn't feel a lot of things, because the emotions that were racing through him were blocking out all the rest.

"Give it to us," Beeker said, still looking out the window. "I want to know what the assignment is and why it's important enough that we're here when we were supposed to be on R&R."

Delilah started to speak. She did it in the voice that always made them feel as if they were in a conference room. "There's a problem here in India that has to be handled, and it has got to be dealt with quickly and effectively."

The moment she started using this tone, any smart man

forgot about the smooth and shapely legs that were showing under her short skirt and took his eyes off her breasts.

"What happened to Cowboy's . . . friend has been going on more and more here in India. It didn't happen because he was one of you. The girl was killed for being with a foreigner. The whole country's being swept up in xenophobic hysteria.

"India is one of the most vital areas in the world. It has the third largest population, enormous natural resources, and a strategic location equal to none."

They'd fallen into it. Beeker had grasped the change in her attitude and their response to her as if it were a life raft. He'd turned, finally, and was looking at her. He could stand this, her being the source, the one who laid out the problem and presented the necessary solutions.

"The country itself is the richest of prizes in global politics. It has been for centuries. For all of history, India has been coveted by the greats. It was the one diamond that escaped Alexander the Great. It was the barrier that, at least partially, withstood the Great Khan and later the militants of Islam. The Chinese have tried to cross the Himalayas for the many centuries, and the French were willing to go to war over India with Britain and Portugal repeatedly. So were the Dutch.

"India is a prize beyond comparison. It's the bait that has caused empires to overextend themselves. It's been the focus of the great superpower showdowns of the past century.

"The British and the Russians were the players at first. We've replaced the British, just the way the Communists in Russia replaced the czars. But we haven't changed the game. It's the same one. It says that ruling India means ruling most of the globe. That's why the capitals of the world tremble whenever the balance of power shifts in this region. When the Soviets invaded Afghanistan—something that Moscow had been planning since the days of the Imperial Russia—Washington was as close to going to war with them as it's ever been.

"When the influence of the Iranian fanatics began to infiltrate the Moslems of Pakistan, both Moscow and Washington started to tremble together.

"That actually is the beginning of our problem."

"*Our* problem?" Beeker asked.

"Yes, Billy Leaps. Ours."

"You want us to go after the Russkies?" Marty Appelbaum said with a gleam in his eyes. "Want us to follow up on Cowboy's stuff, fight with the Afghans. Huh, Del? Is that it? Hey, no sweat. We can go—"

"You may end up working *with* the Russians this time," Delilah said. She was pulling out a new cigarette. To Beeker's disgust, Appelbaum, Harry, and Rosie all moved to light it for her.

"Work with the Commies? Ah, come on, Del. Not that!" Appelbaum had beaten the other men with the matches and was closest to her now.

She puffed on the light and then went on, ignoring his remarks.

"Each new invasion has brought with it a contribution to Indian culture. In many cases it's added to the genius of the country, offering up an element that could be uniquely integrated into the architecture, the arts of the nation.

"But one contribution—unfortunately, the one that the conquerors have been most adamantly interested in forcing on the native peoples—has been to try to convert India to the victor's religion.

"In Goa, for instance, where I met up with Cowboy, there is a strong Roman Catholic presence. The Islamic majority in what is now Pakistan forced the separation of that part of the subcontinent from the Republic of India at the time of independence. India still has a sizable Moslem population, even after the schism. And then there are the Sikhs, a particularly divisive force, one all the more dangerous to the future of India because of their power in the military. They are still the core of the professional fighting force of India, even at a time when Sikh civilians are rioting with astounding regularity.

"Religious strife is almost a given in India. I've only mentioned some of the divisions. There are many more. The stress they put on the country is never-ending. The people have seen it drive them down. They know that the energies of the government are always focused there.

"They see the Islamic revitalization to the west of here, and they worry about its influence. They see the development of Hindu extremism. They see the Sikhs building up private armies. They are very, very tired of it all.

"The Russians are on one doorstep, and the Chinese are on another. Remember, the Chinese have already invaded India once since the Second World War. Here you have the makings of violent xenophobia. When hatred of things foreign is added to the realization that the religious division in the country keeps it from being united, you have a situation where people want something utterly and totally new.

"Did you notice the graffiti on the walls when you were driving in from the airport?"

The question was unexpected. "Yeah," Rosie said; his smile had long before faded away. "It's like any other city. You drive through the poor sections, and there's stuff written on the walls. No big deal."

"But," Delilah went on patiently—too patiently for Beeker, who thought she was beginning to sound like a schoolmarm—"did you read what it said?"

"Just the usual nonsense."

"It wasn't. There's one saying that's written over and over again, more and more frequently, all over the northern half of India: *Akbar Lives!*"

"Hey, yeah, I did see that," Rosie acknowledged. They all nodded a bit. They remembered the slogan.

"Well, gentlemen, you'd better hope to God he doesn't live. And in fact, you're here to make sure that, if he does live, he doesn't survive for long."

She had their complete attention. All the rest had been prelude. They'd learned that about her, how to spot when she was coming to the point.

If it seemed as if she were continuing her diversion, going on with her little historical lecture, they at least had been warned that this was part of the serious stuff.

"In 1575, India was divided up into a mass of small principalities. One of the local leaders, a man we now know as Akbar, was able to conquer many of them and found the first of the great Mogul dynasties. By the time the British arrived in force two hundred years later, the Moguls were still here in Delhi, their capital, although none of his successors was ever as powerful as Akbar.

"When he ascended to his father's throne—which meant little more than becoming the chief of a nomadic tribe—Akbar was the head of an Islamic people. But after his conquests, he found himself ruling an empire of Hindus and Moslems, as well as the followers of many smaller sects.

"Like today, religious division was tearing the country apart. Akbar knew that he couldn't be the emperor of a divided people if he stayed Moslem, not when the Moslems were in the minority.

"Akbar wasn't stupid enough to try to convert his subjects to one of the old religions. That'd been the downfall of many others who'd tried to unite India. Instead, he simply announced that they were all false. They were all only barely tolerated.

"He pronounced instead the Din Illahi as the state religion. It was uniquely Indian and appealed to the emotions and desires of all his people by drawing on many different elements of the old beliefs.

"What Akbar did was to declare himself the head of the religion, as well as the head of state. He was, as much as he was emperor, Khalifa of the Din Illahi. He ruled the temple as well as the palace.

"While he lived and while India worshiped the monotheistic god of the Din Illahi, it experienced unheard-of prosperity and good fortune.

"We'd all thought—all historians have thought—that the episode was an isolated chapter. It was something that Akbar, and only Akbar, had been able to carry off. The religion faded away after his death, though it'd accomplished its purpose by giving the Moguls time to structure a unified state.

"But now we have graffiti announcing that he lives. We have strange rumors of unexplained conspiracies in the Indian government. Almost lost in the tragic religious strife in this country have been all kinds of new attacks on Islamic and Sikh and Hindu temples.

"Someone, gentleman, is trying to take Akbar's place.

"We're reasonably sure that it has nothing to do with the Russians. They're experiencing the same problems in Afghanistan that you know all too well from Vietnam. It's a carbon copy of that war. We also don't think it's a question of the Iranians or other Islamic fanatics working under cover. This would be blasphemy to them. Whoever is proclaiming that Akbar lives is also attacking the idea that Mohammed was a prophet—hardly likely for the Shi'ites to be saying.

"But the conspiracy is here. It's working. It has to be stopped."

"Delilah, I don't want a thing to do with this crap," Beeker said. "I don't touch religious hassles. I don't give a damn about Indian divisions. I want to go home and stay there. This doesn't sound like something for the Berets, not at all."

"It has to be, Billy Leaps." Delilah looked at him with a cold expression. "There's not a whole lot of choice. You see, this isn't a local matter. It's not something we can ignore."

"Why the hell not?" Beak demanded.

"Because about two weeks ago, someone broke into India's center for nuclear research. It's not widely known, but India has the capability of manufacturing small nuclear weapons. They had two of them ready. They're gone.

"I know you'll understand why this mission is so important. You and your men have to find the bombs before they're used."

"How did it happen?" Billy Leaps demanded. "These jokers had to have understood that terrorists might break into those plants. Hell, Delilah, India and Pakistan have fought three wars with one another in the past forty years. They at least had to be prepared to defend their nuclear arsenals against each other."

"Gas." She said the word simply, but it carried an especially obscene sound here in the capital of the country where the Bhopal tragedy had occurred. "A particularly deadly and immediate form of gas appears to have been used.

"There had to have been more involved, of course. Whoever was involved knew too much about where things were kept. They were able to knock out the guards and go into the installation and pick up what they wanted in a matter of minutes. They left in helicopters. The copters were never found."

"How much, Delilah?"

It seemed to surprise her—but only a little bit—that

Roosevelt Boone brought up the question of their payment. The black man usually didn't worry about those things. It must be that he felt a need to cover for Cowboy. The Berets' banker wasn't up to it, obviously.

She sighed, conveying annoyance, as if she'd hoped they were above those considerations by now. "I'll guarantee you a payment of two million dollars if the bombs are returned. But I have a feeling you won't need it."

"Why not?" Rosie asked, obviously intrigued by the answer.

"It seems that whoever is behind this attempted revival of the Din Illahi isn't poor, Rosie. There were messages left on the walls of the nuclear establishment. The messages were the same simple graffiti that you've seen on the streets. With one difference: They were painted on the wall with pure gold."

5

Harry was familiar with the perplexed expression on the ticket agent's face. The same look of panic came over every bureaucrat's face when this happened.

"Look," Harry said softly; he hated making a scene. "Just put down 'Harry Greek.' If you don't, it'll never fit in the space your computer gives you."

The man looked up from his console and seemed for a moment almost paralyzed. Harry was used to this, too. They just didn't like to break the rules. They were so well trained in following orders that they sometimes couldn't even acknowledge the possibility of breaking rules.

"I'm telling you," Harry continued, "it's not going to work any other way. You just cannot get Pappathanassiou into that space. It doesn't work on any airline computer in the world."

The clerk seemed amazed that Harry could even pronounce his own last name. Finally, he shrugged and punched the nickname into the machine. A printed boarding pass came out, and the clerk handed it to Harry. "Mr. Greek," he said. That was also typical. Now that his name was Greek in the machine, it was his real name as far as this functionary was concerned. Well, Harry was finished fighting with these folks.

The clerk went on to the next customer and seemed genuinely relieved when he read his passport. "Mr. T. Beeker." That was easy enough for him to handle. He went through the usual routine and handed the ticket and boarding pass to Tsali. The boy smiled at him and took the papers.

"Let's go, kid," Harry said. He hated dealing with these things. A man goes through war and through the hell of living after war, and then he's got to face numbskulls like this every day! Seems like a man should be able to have his own damned name at least. There shouldn't be anything wrong with that!

He and Tsali walked through the Delhi airport to their gate. Harry scanned the crowded scene. He only semiconsciously checked out the security in the bustling building. He saw that it was much tighter than in most places. It probably would have been in any event, given the terrorist attacks that'd become part of the daily life of India. Since the national government was painfully aware of this Akbar business, they would have made everything all the more secure.

But Harry still saw all the holes. He was trained to do that. He saw which of the guards weren't fully alert, and he noticed that there were three of them in particular whose positions were close together. That was like having a weak spot in a defensive line. As soon as an opponent identified it, that's where he'd send his blockers, and he'd inevitably be able to create a hole big enough for anyone to run through. Harry knew that those guys he'd spotted could be taken out easily. Once they were gone, he could take an entire corridor of the east wing of the airport with no more than three men. He could get some M60s in there and sweep the area clear of civilians in seconds.

Harry would never actually do anything like that. He was

the last man on the earth who'd go after unarmed targets. But he thought that way; he saw those potentials.

They got to the gate for their flight. Harry was all smiles as he watched the stewardess collecting tickets. She was wearing a bright blue sari. Harry loved pretty dresses on women, he really did. He loved women, in fact. He saw the graceful lines of the stewardess's hips through the clinging fabric of the Indian dress, and he wished he could touch the skin underneath. It'd been so long since he'd had it, so very long since he'd made love to a beautiful woman like this one.

He and Tsali were welcomed aboard the jetliner. They took their seats in the first-class section and fastened their seat belts.

Harry was pleased that they were rich enough to fly first class nowadays. Not that he cared about luxury. He and Beeker were the two Black Berets who thought the least of creature comforts in their lives. Harry just liked the legroom. He was well over six feet tall and weighed over two hundred pounds. That was a lot of fighting man to cram into one of those six-abreast configurations in the tourist section. Tsali could've handled that much more easily than the Greek.

Harry looked over and made sure the kid was okay. Now that Tsali was getting so old, he didn't need to be treated like a kid as much. But they were all guilty of falling into the old habit, not just because of his age but because of his inability to speak. They all knew that he'd try to tough it through any situation in the world he found himself in before he'd admit to them that there was a problem.

Everything looked all right with the boy, who was looking out the jetliner's window as usual, fascinated by everything that was going on around him. The plane appeared to be ready to depart. The crew was moving about quickly, seeing to all the last-minute details.

The doors were shut, and the engines revved up. The plane backed away from the terminal and taxied out to the runway. In another few minutes they were in the air.

It amazed Harry how similar this ritual was in every country in the world. That was partly because there were so few kinds of planes that airlines used. This Boeing 727 was certainly the most common. It seemed to be taking over the role the DC-3 had in the old days; it was becoming the workhorse of the air.

If not for the slight hints of strange spices and perfumes, would he have been able to tell the difference between this flight and one in the United States? They were all the same, and even if the food they'd be served was a little exotic, there'd be a familiarity to the meal because, he was sure, it'd be served on the same small plastic tray that he'd have eaten off of if this were a Delta flight to Chicago.

There were lots of things that stayed the same, no matter where you were. The way he was attracted to the stewardess as she moved up and down the aisles was another.

Then Harry felt it. He closed his eyes tightly, as if in sudden pain. The woman was close by and talking softly to another passenger. She'd probably be here soon and ask him if he wanted something to drink. The cocktail in the little bottle wouldn't be any different here from what it would've been in Illinois. But that wasn't a pleasant idea anymore.

Harry wasn't like the other Black Berets. He liked females the way they did, that was for sure. But he didn't look at every one of them as if she were a wonderful possibility. Especially not after having heard Cowboy's story. Women were something he'd rather avoid. He couldn't think about how much pleasure they could bring, not now. He could only contemplate the pain.

To know a woman in the intimate way Cowboy'd known

Carmelita, even just once, and then to see that kind of picture of her—Harry shuddered at the thought. He'd known other women who'd died after they'd been lovers of Black Berets. There'd been women he'd loved, and they'd been the real losers in the end. He never wanted to know that pain again, that loss and that sense of guilt.

He'd seen it on Cowboy's face in the hotel suite. There was nothing you could do after someone was gone that way. There was no way to say you were sorry that could count, and there was no way you could make up for the loss.

Harry put a hand to his forehead, as if he could wipe away the hurt that was flooding his brain. That's what women really meant to a man like Harry: hurt. The kind that doesn't go away for a long time—maybe for his entire life.

He felt Tsali's hand on his forearm and willed himself not to show what he was feeling—at least not to Tsali. He forced himself to smile at the kid. Then the stewardess was there. That was good, too. She might've misunderstood the way he could've reacted to her before. Now he could just take his smile and aim it in her direction. Just be a businessman on a trip, make everyone feel good, don't make any waves.

He ordered Cokes for them both. Then he reclined his seat back and thought, not about his personal demons, but about the events that they'd walked into and his upcoming role in trying to sort them out.

They were on their way to Bombay. It wasn't the first time Harry's ancestry had come in handy on one of their missions. He looked every inch of his Greek heritage. He had that strong Greek nose, the thick dark hair, and the dark shadow of a beard that always showed, even after he'd shaved. His skin had an olive complexion.

Modern Greeks were some of the most voracious traders

in the world. Since classical times, wherever there had been a marketplace, the Greeks were in residence.

The Berets needed information on trading going on in India, and they needed it fast. They couldn't trust the Indian government to know what had to be discovered, and they certainly weren't going to wait for the lethargic Delhi bureaucracy to bring forth the data. They didn't have to. They could send Harry off to get it for them, passing him off as a respected member of a large Greek shipping family from Salonika. It was an airtight cover.

Tsali was just frosting on the cake. Not in terms of Harry's story; Tsali didn't serve a good purpose in that regard. But they knew that the Greek would enjoy himself more if he had the kid with him and that he'd complain less about things if Tsali were his companion.

The place where Harry was told he'd find the information was Bombay. He knew a little about the city. It had actually begun as a British trading post. The island that had been the site of the original English settlement was now surrounded by one of the largest municipalities in the world. It was the financial heart of India.

The plane made the journey in about the time it would've taken to fly from Chicago to Shreveport, Harry figured. Even the landing was the same as if they'd been in the States. The accordion gateway that snaked out from the terminal of Santa Cruz Airport was just as familiar.

But as soon as they walked out of the air-conditioned terminal and into the streets of the city, there was no doubt they were in a foreign land. The heat was incredible, even to Harry, who'd spent so many years in Nam. And it was at least as humid as Indochina had been. Hirsute men like Harry sweat a lot; when they walked out of the building, he could feel his body fluids drench his clothing almost immediately.

They climbed into a cab, choosing one at random from the hawking cabbies lined up outside the door. They had only their hand luggage—all they'd need—and were able to avoid the crowds of passengers lined up to retrieve their suitcases, as well as the hordes of official and unofficial porters desperately trying to earn a few rupees by carrying them.

Harry gave the driver an address, and they were off.

Usually an airport gives you at least a middle-class view of a city. You get to see miles of pleasant suburbs, or else riverfront—something like that. In Boston, Harry remembered, you looked out the window of your plane right onto downtown, and he, like every other traveler, left that city with an image of modern skyscrapers rising out of brick-colored historic sections. Maybe other cities weren't all that pretty—he remembered a ride from LaGuardia to midtown Manhattan that went through East Harlem—but never had there been, in all his years of travel, any ride as devastating as the ride from the airport to Bombay.

It was at least partially that heat. Harry had unbuttoned his shirt as soon as the cab started moving. It wasn't that he thought he could escape it by undoing his clothing, but he was desperate even for the slight breeze caused by the movement of the car to hit his skin. Tsali, he saw, did the same. The kid didn't have Harry's hairiness, and he usually wasn't bothered by temperature. But now he was hanging his head out the window, directing the breeze onto his bare neck, as if he were a little boy again.

What ever could it be like to live in weather like this? Harry wondered. And in such utter poverty! Calcutta was supposed to be the center of destitution. Harry knew all about Mother Teresa and her work there. How could it possibly surpass this?

Soon the taxi was navigating toward the hotel where they were staying. They got out, and a uniformed doorman came over to pick up their small pieces of luggage. He insisted on carrying them and became offended when Harry indicated that the two Americans could have done it themselves.

Walking through the hotel was another time warp. Just as the plane had made him think he was on a regular jaunt in the States, this place could have been in center city Philadelphia. It was modern, sleekly designed, and touched up with details that seemed to have come out of some decorators' guidebook published in Peoria. Nothing here told him that he was in India.

Nor did anything here make him remember that there were hungry bodies out in the street. They were taken to their suite by another uniformed lackey. Harry tipped him and then studied the two matching king-size beds that dominated the room. Tsali went over and flipped on the color television. He couldn't hear the sounds coming out of the device; he was comforted simply by the sight of a favorite cowboy show.

Harry felt as if someone were playing tricks on him, sending him back and forth between different realities. The air conditioning was on full blast here. He had to button his shirt back up. It all made him feel claustrophobic.

He got Tsali's attention so that the kid could read his lips. "Let's go. Let's go find this Mr. Batliwalla and start our business."

Tsali gestured to him that he was surprised that Harry wanted to move right away, not even take a shower. But Harry knew that a shower now wouldn't do much good. Maybe just before they turned in for the night, but not now. He wanted to go out. What he really meant was that he had to leave this artificial atmosphere. He couldn't stand to be here, in this plastic imitation of a hotel. He wanted to see the real India.

Tsali didn't argue. He turned off the television, and the two of them went back to the elevators, back to the streets of Bombay.

The smells that came up from the streets where they were walking nearly made Harry gag. He saw the filth of the clothes on the children and the women, and he saw the ramshackle huts they lived in off the side of the road.

How could men do this to other people? he wondered. And how did these people survive? They were far from the pseudo-American comforts of their hotel. They'd stopped a couple different policemen, making sure they were headed in the correct direction.

The teeming throngs of people seemed to be a living mass in this part of Bombay. They functioned not so much as individuals but as a whole, a living thing that sometimes seemed so powerful, it made Harry think it could consume him.

He wouldn't have been surprised. Not after how he'd seen them living, packed into the smallest shacks imaginable and eating . . .

Even with the breeze from the ocean, the smell of stale fish clung to the air. It was an almost physical presence. Poor people living in a seaport eating a diet of seafood were no surprise to Harry. He remembered the diets of the Vietnamese and the ingenious ways they'd learned to cook their ocean harvests. But this was different.

The women squatted by boiling cauldrons of oil in which they were frying food right on the streets of Bombay. There was plenty of fish here; the shore was only blocks away. But what was left for these poverty-stricken people wasn't fit for human consumption.

Harry looked down and saw the eyes of a dozen small, foul-smelling beasts staring up at him from one pot. At that moment the woman lifted up a piece to feed to a small boy. But the meat she'd retrieved wasn't fish. It was a small rat that had jumped into the boiling oil and drowned. The woman held it for a full beat of time, as if she were reluctant to throw it away. Harry stood terrified for that moment, unwilling to believe that she could even think of such a thing.

She finally tossed the dead rat aside. But the stew was obviously too valuable to be wasted. He'd have thought she'd throw out the whole potful after it'd been contaminated by the rodent. But she simply reached back into it with her utensil and once again searched for something to feed the squalling young boy.

Harry lost it then.

A small swarm of little street kids had been following the well-dressed tourists ever since they'd gotten out of the taxi. Their number had increased as the trip continued. They were used to hitting up the few travelers who strayed here, obviously. But they were just as used to not getting anything from them. Harry had dealt with beggars in countries all over the world, and even he'd learned to ignore their pleas. But not after he saw that rat in the food.

These were pros at the game. They were only going through the motions with Harry and Tsali. They knew that the older English *memsahibs* who got lost and scared were good for the handouts.

But Harry probably started a small myth all by himself that afternoon. He made sure that every big, dark-haired Western tourist would be a major mark for the beggars of Bombay for a long time.

Harry stopped in the middle of a crowded street and turned to face the pack of begging youngsters. At first they must have thought he was going to do them some harm. They all took a step backward. But he didn't make a move on them. Instead, he simply opened up his wallet and extended it toward the hands of the ravenous kids. "Take it," he said, hoping the message would be universal if they couldn't speak English. "Take all of it."

Tsali knew that he could have stopped him. But he didn't try. He'd grown up with these strange men who were, each in his own way, his fathers. He'd learned to love each one for the strange things he did. Harry did things like this every once in a while. That was his way. Tsali just stood and watched, hoping Harry was getting some good feeling out of it for himself.

And Harry was obviously feeling better about something as he watched the small brown hands of the beggars hunt through the open wallet and take out the multicolored Indian bills. There was more money in there than those kids would earn in a lifetime. Some of them couldn't even identify the larger denominations and held them up to the light as if to find evidence that this largesse was real.

Tsali didn't mind, because there was plenty of money in his own wallet, and he knew that Harry had the same collection of credit cards that he himself carried. Beeker would have scowled at the scene, and Cowboy would've been furious. Tsali was simply pleased that Harry was finding some pleasure.

The kids fled like thieves as soon as they'd picked the wallet clean. They acted as if they were sure they'd end up in jail if they were caught. With a prize like the one they'd just found, they couldn't imagine that the man involved wasn't going to turn them in right away. This kind of thing had to be a setup— that's all there was to it.

Tsali smiled when he saw that, and he understood what was happening. He took Harry's shirt sleeve and gently tugged it, leading the Greek back on their way.

6

When a man trained for war is in a strange environment, his body is always on the alert. A truly trained soldier is never at rest. But more than that, when a disciplined soldier is in an alien land, his senses pick up danger that no one else would notice.

Even while he was descending into depression from seeing the poverty around him, something kept Harry alert enough to respond to a single flicker of bright light.

Tsali saw it as well.

They moved so quickly and in such harmony that it seemed as if they were dancers going through an often-rehearsed duet together. In a sense they were.

Because of the speed of their movements away from one another, which left them both facing the dimly lit alleyway, the knives cutting through the air around them didn't hit home. Those daggers had been aimed at them, there was no question about it.

There was no time to ask why. There was only a chance that they might survive whoever and whatever was assailing them.

Harry reached into the holster hidden underneath the loose

waistband of his slacks. Tsali went through the same motions. When their hands came free, each carried a compact Colt pistol. They were the Mustang model, small stainless-steel guns that were only five and a half inches long; their barrels measured only about two and three-quarter inches. But the Colt carried five 9-millimeter rounds in its magazine.

They'd learned to value the Colt Mustang for its small size and the ease with which they could conceal it. Whoever was attacking them hadn't had a hint that they'd be armed, that was for sure. But the Black Berets were always armed when they went into strange territory.

The assassins were too brave for their own good. They'd seen Harry and Tsali as defenseless merchants, as tourists weak enough to give alms to begging children—easy marks. The two had been lucky to escape the first knife assault, that was all. Now the murderers would finish them off at close hand.

Four of them leaped out of their hiding places. Each of them had another blade in his hand. The steel reflected even more light now that they were in the open. The streets might be crowded, but no one would bother to report an assault in this section.

The evidence of that was all around them. The people who'd so recently been crowding them had moved back, creating an arena in the middle of the busy district, with human bodies for walls. The women moved away from the altercation; a few smart men did the same; the rest of the men, along with all the boys, stayed to watch the battle.

Life's cheap in a place like the slums of Bombay. The onlookers felt little horror that people were fighting, the foreigners with handguns and the others with knives. There was no more excitement than there would have been at a cockfight. When it was over, the onlookers would melt away no matter who won. They didn't even bother to cheer for one side or the other.

But the assassins weren't about to melt away. They rushed toward Harry and Tsali; then the Mustangs blasted out their bullets. Those little packages carried big payoffs. The two men nearest to Harry went down, a single bullet apiece in each forehead.

At his side, Harry heard Tsali's pistol bark out. One body collapsed in midflight, it seemed. It'd been on its way toward Harry, led by a gleaming steel dagger. But a bullet caught it in the chest, throwing its trajectory off, and a small 9-millimeter slug sent it into a spiral.

That's the way you think in the middle of battle. It doesn't matter if it's in the streets of Bombay or in the jungles of Cambodia. You don't think about men who are coming at you; you think about their bodies as things that are threatening your life, or else you think about the weapons they're carrying with them. You do that so you don't flinch, the way you do when you see a mother debating whether to feed her baby a dead rat.

Four shots had been fired—that was all. There was a sudden stop to the hubbub that'd been swirling around them. The street peddlers stopped their cries, children stopped squalling, mothers stopped nagging. The scene froze. Harry and Tsali waited to see if there were going to be more assailants. Each only had three bullets left in his magazine. Both knew that. Three each—for how many attackers?

But then the noise of the city came back to life. It began when a single infant resumed its angry monologue. As if that were their cue, the rest of the people began to move and speak, laugh and yell, and return to the exotic and poverty-stricken street scene.

Harry looked at Tsali and nodded. As soon as the younger man saw the Greek put the pistol back into the hidden holster that hugged just beneath his hips, the Cherokee boy did the same thing. They waited to see what would happen next.

A man walked up to them and made a small gesture, bowing his head with his hands folded in front of him. "You are the men from Salonika, sir?" he asked.

"Yes," Harry said. Every inch of his body was ready to spring if he needed to move.

The man made another gesture, and suddenly a group of scantily clad men rushed not at the Americans but toward the dead bodies. Harry figured at first that they were after whatever might have been valuable and hidden on the assassins. He thought he was right when he saw the knives being collected and pocketed and the clothing on the corpses being searched.

But that wasn't their only purpose. As soon as they were finished scavenging, they moved the four men back toward the alley from where they'd attacked.

"You will come with me, *sahib*?" their new guide said. "Mr. Batliwalla awaits you."

"Most inconvenient for you, Mr. Pappathanassiou." The man who'd been introduced as Mr. Batliwalla was sitting in a comfortable chair in a reception room off his office. Harry was surprised at how easily he pronounced the complicated Greek name. "I am pleased, however, that you were wise enough to prepare yourself. A man unarmed in these times is a fool. You, I'm told, are no fool."

A servant was passing around cups of tea. Harry and Tsali each took one and, following Mr. Batliwalla's example, sipped the rich brew. It was so unlike the tea they were used to occasionally tasting in the States that it seemed wrong even to call it by the same name. The buffalo milk gave it a distinct flavor, as well.

Mr. Batliwalla wasn't going to talk while the servant was in the room. Only when the three of them were left alone did he begin again.

"These are very difficult times for any of us who are not members of the native races of India. We are less welcome than ever before, and I assure you, sirs, that we have never been all that welcome in any event."

Tsali spoke with his hands. Harry translated. "My young friend thought you were Indian yourself."

Mr. Batliwalla smiled at Tsali. "I am Parsi. We are a people who have been in India for centuries. Since so many others have come here since our own arrival, we might well claim a superior right to use the appellation 'Indian.' But we are a race apart.

"We came to this part of India when Islam conquered our native land, Persia! We are followers of Zoroaster. We worship the sun." Mr. Batliwalla pointed to a brilliant bas relief constructed from beaten gold that hung from the wall and that obviously represented the natural life source. "We have been here, the few thousands of us who survive, since just after the time of Mohammed.

"But we are a separate people. Like your own, we are a commercial people. India, although an adopted home, has been good to us."

"I understand that," Harry said, indicating that he'd asked for the explanation only for the boy's sake. Mr. Batliwalla nodded. "My people know your trading brilliance very well."

"The Parsi and the Greeks have been partners in commerce since Alexander, sir. You are welcome in my house, as your ancestors were welcome in my ancestors' homes."

"You're very gracious, Mr. Batliwalla."

"A slight cost when one is contemplating an . . . *interesting* business acquaintance, Mr. Pappathanassiou."

Harry figured the man was about fifty, but he wasn't sure. The complexion had been carefully cared for. It was lighter than that of most Indians he'd seen—not much different from his own, in fact. The eyes were dark brown, and the man's body was stouter than those of the men on the streets of Bombay, although he was not fat. Only a few years ago, Harry speculated, Mr. Batliwalla had been a very well-built man.

"Your firm, I understand, is interested in trading with India?" Mr. Batliwalla asked.

"Yes."

"You do well to search out a Parsi. One of the many reasons we have done well in India is the utter inability of the other peoples here to understand the wonders of commerce. One can never tell, for instance, when one of the Brahmins, the upper-caste Hindus, will go off on a fanatical religious quest.

"Take Gandhi, a man with a good education and a potentially successful future in the law. The next thing you knew, he was dressed in rags and playing at being a saint." The disgust with which Mr. Batliwalla spoke made it obvious that he thought it a sin that the great peacemaker hadn't founded a law firm. "Fortunately, you're dealing with a Parsi. What is your interest in India?"

"There are many possibilities," Harry said, only slowly moving into the subject, the way a real commercial person would. This was a high-stake game of poker, Harry realized. You didn't start by announcing your hand's contents. "There are many opportunities here in such a large country."

"I hope your interest is in computers, sir." Mr. Batliwalla said that quickly and emphatically. The excitement in his voice about high-tech trade was shocking in this room full of ancient artifacts, so clearly adored by the man.

Mr. Batliwalla continued quickly when he realized Harry wasn't going to pick up the conversation. "India has ridiculous new laws about foreign investment: The Delhi government is overly concerned with foreign ownership of the country, a hangover from the colonial days. The only exception is computers. That's the one place where a foreigner can enter the market and still control a majority of his own firm's ownership.

"God knows this place needs the infernal machines," Mr. Batliwalla went on. "The telephone systems and anything approaching modern communications are in desperate need of overhaul in India. There's a fortune to be made here."

"Actually," Harry said, leaning forward, "I was thinking more about . . . gold."

Mr. Batliwalla's face changed its expression entirely. The excitement that the computer talk had produced was gone. Now came a shrewder look. This was a conversation he'd had before, often.

"The plague of India," Mr. Batliwalla intoned.

Tsali looked puzzled. The Parsi trader caught that and explained, "The Indians have lived through innumerable invasions, my son. They are used to war; it is their dark heritage. Whenever foreign armies haven't been poised to invade, they fight one another.

"The common man here has learned not to trust anything but gold. It is the one thing that will not lose its value in wartime—in fact, it will become more precious. He has learned not to hope for investments, either. Investments take time and peace to be nurtured. He doesn't believe he can look forward to either in India.

"He can only look forward to invasion and civil disruption. So he hoards gold. Over the ages, the results have been disastrous. You see, gold can give you the security that you have something—if you can hide it from the invader. There is no doubt about that.

"But in the years that you hold it, nothing happens to the gold. It doesn't increase in volume. It doesn't produce offspring. It doesn't create interest. It sits there.

"Even the most primitive African tribesman measures his real wealth with cattle. There's milk you can have regularly from the females. The bulls mate with the cows, and there are children. There's sense to having cattle as a measure of wealth.

"But gold is only to be hoarded. Here in India the government's industrialization plans are ruined, at least partially, because whenever there is manufacture that's sent off to foreign markets, the income is spent on gold, not reinvested in new plants.

"India's hunger for gold is immense, never-ending, and unquenchable. If you have it, sir"—Mr. Batliwalla had turned back to Harry—"this is the place to sell it, there is no doubt."

"I was actually thinking that I might want to do just that. There are the problems with customs—"

"A bother," Mr. Batliwalla agreed. "But certainly there are ways that that can be overcome."

"The real problem," Harry went on, "is to find the buyer."

"But there is always a buyer, Mr. Pappathanassiou."

"For twenty-two-troy pounds of bullion?"

Not even centuries of Parsi trading skill could hold back Mr. Batliwalla's astonishment. He mumbled the figure once without even verifying it with Harry. Rather, it seemed that he was trying to fit the sum on for size. Then he did some quick calculations. "That's worth about one hundred million of your American dollars."

"About," Harry agreed, sipping the last of his tea.

"We would have to find someone with great resources."

"You must know who that would be," Harry said, standing up. "You are, they tell me, the greatest merchant in Bombay. Certainly if anyone could unload that many pounds of gold, it would be you."

"The deal of the century," Mr. Batliwalla said. "My children's children's children would talk about it." It was clear that he thought this lifetime accomplishment of his would put him on a par with Gandhi. Mr. Batliwalla came back to the present. "We will meet soon, Mr. Pappathanassiou. I will call you at your hotel."

7

Mr. Batliwalla was knocking on their hotel room door in less than twenty-four hours. He waved to his guards to wait for him outside in the corridor and walked into the room upon Harry's invitation.

In the background the television was on.

Mr. Batliwalla didn't have to look to see why Harry was watching the special news report. "The Oberoi Hotel bombing," he said. "It is a bad thing, terrible. The government had been able to distract the notice of the foreign journalists up to now. The attacks on tourists and visiting businessmen were made to look like isolated events. But this catastrophe will bring the eyes of the world down upon us."

They moved together toward the screen. The terrorist act had killed over thirty people, over half of them American and British. Bodies littered the sidewalks outside the building. There was still smoke rising in the background.

"The Delhi government cannot absorb many more of these shocks. Every day one hears about a new disturbance. To an extent, it seems that people will accept things as the usual if they see and hear about them often enough." Mr. Batliwalla's eyes never left the television. "But there must be an end somewhere to all of this. If the violence is truly aimed at outsiders, the standing of the government in the world will be damaged. India quakes, Mr. Pappathanassiou. If the government cannot contain the violence, if it cannot keep it from spreading, then we are in grave danger.

"India without Delhi in control would be unthinkable. It would mean the destruction of the Indian state. In its place would rise up dozens of tiny principalities. We would be disintegrated into local units as we haven't been since the time of the Moguls."

Harry reached over and turned off the machine. He offered Mr. Batliwalla a seat and then took one facing him. Tsali stood politely and attentively behind him. "You have news for me?"

Mr. Batliwalla responded to Harry's return to the business at hand. His concern for Indian politics disappeared. There was money to be made here.

"I do. There is the question of a small payment. Of course I assume you expect that I, as the middleman—"

"You'll be handsomely rewarded," Harry said, shutting off this conversation about a commission. "That's always been assumed."

"It will have to be limited to what you call a finder's fee," Mr. Batliwalla said. "I'm afraid I can do no more than introduce you. I've told my contacts of your possible interests. They wish to meet with you. But they insist on doing it themselves."

"I expected that," Harry said.

"I must tell you that the people with whom you are going to meet are of the most suspicious sort. You obviously had reasons for not dealing with the Bank of India, Mr. Pappathanassiou. That limits our possibilities."

"There's no need to play these games, Mr. Batliwalla. I obviously don't want any government to know what I'm doing."

"We won't deal, then, with the source of your gold."

"You're right." Harry smiled. "We won't discuss it at all." He'd always meant to let the man assume the bullion was stolen or had been gotten through some other illegal means, perhaps in payment for an illicit deal of some kind.

"Then you must leave Bombay. I will tell you about your next step, but I must advise you, sir, that the current unrest in India is only making your holdings more valuable with every day that passes. Indians believe less and less in the stability of the Delhi government—we've just seen the reasons why. They're rushing to redeem their paper currency for bullion, forcing the price up every hour. If you were to sell now, you would find that your gold is worth much more in only a matter of days.

"If this crisis does in fact throw India into civil war, then there is little hope."

"I have need to get rid of the bullion, Mr. Batliwalla. I want the money to be paid into a Swiss account of mine in British pounds. I have my own reasons for wanting to hurry. But why are you warning me about your associates? Are they untrustworthy businessmen?"

Mr. Batliwalla was obviously perplexed. He hesitated, seeming to choose his words carefully. "My associates are not even businessmen, Mr. Pappathanassiou. That is my concern. I am, to be frank, shocked by who they are.

"They are a prominent Brahmin family, one that can trace its prominence back to the days of the first Moguls. Some of their younger sons and daughters, in fact, have taken up the European custom of trying to establish that they are the descendants of ancient nobility. I'd always dismissed their silliness as just an attempt on their part to make their way into the jet set of the West.

"But the Patchels are evidently not as frivolous as I had thought. They are amassing large landholdings in the Deccan, in the south. But they are still headquartered at the family residence, not far from Delhi. That's where you are to go. They will meet you there."

"You said they claim to be the descendants of ancient nobles?"

"Yes," Mr. Batliwalla said. He may have appreciated the mercantilism that this Patchel family was displaying, but that element of their lives wasn't impressive to him. "They insist that they are the modern heirs to the ancient Mogul emperors, in fact. They claim"—Mr. Batliwalla smiled tolerantly—"that they are the descendants of Akbar the Great. Ridiculous!" Mr. Batliwalla stood up and prepared to take his leave.

Harry also stood and offered his hand in a Western handshake. Mr. Batliwalla accepted the gesture.

"The Patchels." Delilah spoke the family's name as if she were trying it on for size, to see if it sounded at all credible. "I met one of their sons recently in Cannes."

Beeker was seated calmly in a chair in the Delhi hotel room. The moment Delilah spoke of her being on the French Riviera, his posture stiffened. Tsali saw it and fought to keep back a smile. When he was growing up, he had found these games of the adults increasingly humorous. But where his father was concerned, he couldn't dismiss anything that hinted of danger. He hoped now that no one else had seen Billy Leaps's reaction. He would never want anyone else to see weakness in his father.

"He was innocuous," Delilah went on. "A flighty thing, really. But there was something more to him, something I couldn't put my finger on then, or now." Her frown came and went. "But that doesn't mean that the rest of the clan is that way. In a new democracy—India's still that; the government here is less than forty years old—the presence of a royal claim to a throne is dangerous.

"We always think in terms of revolutions coming from the left, from Communists. But if a member of the Patchel family can convince the common people of India that he's the real heir to the Mogul throne . . ."

"What do we do?" Cowboy asked. "Sit here and wonder about it? We don't have any other clues. And the whole thing's getting pretty heavy. It's only coincidence that Harry and Tsali's hotel wasn't the one blown up."

Tsali saw his father react physically once more. He felt a strange emotion, one he couldn't really identify, when he again saw proof that his father cared so much about him, even as much as he would about a woman he loved. It gave him a sense of invulnerability, he supposed. When your father is on your side, what danger can threaten you?

"We can't all go down there to Agra, where they live," Beeker announced. "But we need more than just one man at the same time.

"Harry's got the introduction. He's the big-time Greek gold trader they're expecting. That's fine. We'll run with it. I'm going with him. The rest of you can try to learn what you can here.

"Delilah, don't you have any contacts in the Indian government or military that we can use?" His tone told her that he knew she did.

She nodded.

"Okay," Beeker continued, "Marty and Cowboy and Rosie, you three—and Tsali—you find out what you can here in Delhi. I'm going to Agra with Harry."

Tsali's hands flew through the air. He moved them so quickly that Beeker had trouble following his sign language.

"The kid's got you," Cowboy said, speaking in the same laconic voice that he'd had since seeing those pictures of Carmelita. He had learned Tsali's communicative gestures most fluently and often took on the role of translator when his extra skill was needed. "The contacts we've had so far have seen him with Harry. They might get suspicious if he disappeared and you were in his place.

"You can be added," Cowboy continued his quick translation. "But he can't be taken away."

Beeker nodded quickly. "Fine. The kid can come with me. But the rest of you, get moving on this end. Fast."

Tsali was amazed. The scene he was now part of was something out of most schoolboys' fantasies. He stood back from the gathering, not wanting to intrude on it, wanting only to be able to remember it just as he saw it now.

The people were all elegantly dressed. They were drinking out of crystal glasses and moving around in formal postures, just the way they did in movies.

His father stood over on the other side of the patio, dressed as Tsali had never seen him. Billy Leaps Beeker, of all men, was clothed in a tropical-weight tuxedo. He looked unbearably uncomfortable in it, even though the fabric must have been light.

There were three men playing sitars over in another corner. Tsali was disappointed that he couldn't hear the music that came from the stringed instruments. He was sure it would only have added to the exotic nature of the party.

He watched as a beautiful woman approached Beeker. Like any adolescent boy, Tsali thought he himself was too awkward to handle females well. He got nervous and tense whenever they got too close to him. Even though he had had wonderful adventures when Cowboy had taken him to erotic establishments, he was afraid he could never seduce a girl on his own.

That is, not unless he could pick up lessons from Beeker. Tsali was inordinately proud of how women flocked to his father. They sensed the military bearing of the man. They were attracted by his dark hair and the blue eyes that seemed so out of place against his brown skin. Those eyes, Tsali knew, were the result of Beeker's father having married a white woman. They were the only thing that Beeker had of hers. She'd left him alone with his grandmother when he was only a baby and had gone off to lose herself in bars and dives.

That would never happen to him, Tsali knew. After a childhood of aloneness, he was now part of this group called the Black Berets. They would never willingly go away and make him rebuild his life, not after all they knew he'd gone through.

He remembered all of it—the foster families, the institutions for orphans and for the physically handicapped. That would never happen again. The only way the Black Berets would ever leave would be if they finally met the warrior's fate—if they died in battle.

But Tsali was here with them this time, as he'd been with them on most of their recent adventures. He wasn't worried about losing these five men who were his family now. Because he knew that if they were to die the honorable death of the soldier in battle, he would be with them, and he would die, too. And to die for his father's cause would be infinitely better than to live without that man.

But Tsali didn't linger on those thoughts. He actually refused to believe that the Black Berets could be beaten in anything by anyone. It certainly seemed, he thought with a smile as he saw how the beautiful woman was talking to his father, that no girl was ever going to get the best of them. At least that wouldn't happen.

She was wearing the strange pants that he'd seen on many Indian women, both rich and poor. The pants were tight at the ankles and up the calves but then floated out to become loose for the rest of the body.

Rosie had told them those were called *kurta pajama*: that that was where the English word for nighttime garments had come from. That made Tsali break into a silent giggle. He liked the idea of his father talking to a woman who was already dressed for bed. Beeker, he thought with pride, usually managed to get the ones he wanted there in the end.

Well, sometimes, at least. Maybe not as often as Rosie and Cowboy did. Tsali realized—and respected—that Billy Leaps really only wanted to do that with Delilah. Even though the beautiful blonde woman made him mad so often, that was the woman he wanted the most. And deep down inside, deeper than his adolescent pride at how easily Beeker got other women, he hoped that Delilah would win every time. Because as much as he loved this life of his now, he had another dream; that she would come to their farm in Louisiana and live with them, giving him still more proof that his loneliness was over.

But those were a child's dreams, he told himself quickly. It was time to give those up. Better to start thinking about himself as a man whom one of these women might want for himself. Better to do that than worry about what that woman might be saying to Billy Leaps Beeker. Tsali tried to stand up straight, to make his eyes seem like the sharp eagles' eyes that Beeker had. He didn't want to conquer women the way Rosie did, nor did he want to play the seduction games that were Cowboy's second nature. Tsali wanted to be like Billy Leaps now. He wanted women to come to him.

"But you aren't Greek, obviously, Mr. Basalo." The woman had introduced herself as Nur Patchel. She was holding an unlit cigarette in her hand, waving it toward Beeker, obviously expecting him to light it.

Beeker hated this; it was the kind of shit that Cowboy could pull off, but not he. It was part of the assignment, though. He'd have to play out the charade that he was a playboy investor. He picked up a lighter from a table nearby and flicked its flame on. He held it out, but not far enough that she didn't have to move a little bit toward him to get her cigarette going.

She inhaled deeply—theatrically, in fact. Then she let the smoke flow out of her mouth and her nostrils. His eyes trailed over her body. The *kurta pajama* was made from silk so sheer, it was almost translucent.

The top was also a take on a traditional Indian tunic. Its fabric was heavier; but then, with her breasts, there was no need for a man to actually see how sexual that part of her body was.

"No," he finally answered, "I'm not. I'm Venezuelan."

"But your English is perfect!"

"I went to Annapolis," he lied. It was a good cover. God knew that after years in the Marine Corps, Billy Leaps Beeker knew enough about the Naval Academy's teachings to pull it off. The Venezuelan connection had been decided on to give him a handle that would get him into this secret world of million-dollar trades. He was, so the story would go, a member of a South American oil family who were in partnership with Harry's Greeks. Many Latin oligarchs had their sons educated in the United States. Beeker's Spanish was so good that, if anyone ever really disbelieved his story, he could use that to prove himself.

"Interesting," Nur said. She didn't seem to question his line at all. He wondered what her part in all of this was.

"My father will be having some dealings with you in the morning, I understand."

"Yes."

She didn't seem to want to pursue the subject. She was

probably, he decided, not important in this scheme. She was just a woman who was pampered and indulged by a rich daddy. He'd seen plenty of them in his life.

"I hope you enjoy our party. It's not often that we entertain. That will change soon."

He took that as proof that his take on her was right. Here she was, caught in a provincial city far from the bright lights of Delhi, just waiting for her papa to make a killing so her hostessing could be better appreciated.

"I loathe having so many tradesmen here," she went on. Then she quickly moved to make sure that Beeker wasn't offended. "Not you, of course, Mr. Basalo. You are indeed most welcome." That set him on edge. There was something in her voice that was unexpected. She wasn't indulging in a slight flirtation now; this was somehow serious business.

"But my father, for the time being, feels a need to make these people feel welcome in our home. In time"—her neck stiffened and her head took on a haughty pose—"they won't be necessary for us."

She quickly changed her stance, as if she realized he might have seen something that he shouldn't have. "But Mr. Basalo, you have such exciting business with us."

How much did she know? he wondered.

"It is the kind of business, in fact, that should have a special preparation, don't you think? It would be a shame"—she sipped her champagne as a punctuation mark to increase the tension she obviously hoped was developing between them—"to limit my family's and your dealings to the dreariness of the conference table."

Beeker couldn't believe how this woman was coming on to him. What was her game? He hated the idea of studding for information, but something told him that this was one time he should do it. She did know more than he'd thought—he was sure of it now. Information was power, and he was never one to go into any potential conflict without all the armament he could muster up.

He smiled at her—a slight gesture, but one that, coming from Beeker, usually had the desired effect on a woman. She seemed to respond. "Yes, I see that you agree. The party can go on without us, don't you think?"

Tsali watched the two of them leave the party. He took another glass of wine from the tray of a passing waiter. He didn't mind wearing this tuxedo. He liked this moment of sham sophistication. He'd never admit that to his father; but then he'd probably never have to. Tsali knew that Beeker would never suspect that the kid would enjoy this.

Tsali had another silent smile as he wondered if Beeker suspected that the boy wanted to have beautiful women in pajamas escort him out of cocktail parties when he grew up. He'd never disillusion Billy Leaps about that either, he knew.

He walked into the center of the party now, toward Harry. He tried to make his movements as masterful as Beeker's. He'd learned so much else from this adopted father; why not that as well?

8

Nur Patchel was lying on her side on the large free-standing bed that dominated the center of her room. Her tunic had fallen open, and only a sheer, brassierelike garment covered her breasts.

She was waiting for Beeker to undress. This was not, he'd learned, a woman who waited. She wanted to bed him tonight, before the negotiations for the gold sale in the morning. He figured that she thought she might be able to secure an upper hand in the business conversations if they had sex first. It wasn't a sure thing; he wasn't that taken with her sexuality. But for her it was worth a try.

Beeker pulled off his suit jacket. He undid his bow tie. As he was undoing his cuff links, he suddenly realized that she wasn't moving. He'd expected her to undress at the same time. But she stayed on the bed and watched him, like a monarch who expected this diversion from one of her subjects. He pulled the shirt off and watched her appraise him.

She was pleased. She lifted an eyebrow to indicate her heightened interest.

He never used to think of his body as erotic. Then he'd met

Delilah, and she'd shown him how much a woman could appreciate a male . . .

Oh, no, he wasn't going to think of her now. He kept his mind on Nur and her hungry expression. He kicked off his shoes and bent down to pull off his socks. Then he stood back up and unbuckled his belt and unzipped his fly. His pants fell to the floor, and he was in his shorts.

There was no way to hide his physical response to the beautiful woman. He didn't want to deny it, anyway. He wanted to do something about it. The first step was to get rid of the shorts. He put his thumbs under the elastic and pushed down.

He moved over to her bed and leaned over. He took Nur in his arms and lifted her halfway off the mattress. She hadn't expected that. And she was also surprised that his kiss was as hard as other parts of his body right then. His tongue went inside her mouth, and its tip explored and tasted her.

Her arms resisted in the beginning; at first, she tried to push him away. But he answered her feeble shoves by falling down onto the bed with her body under his. His legs were moving then, spreading hers apart. Then her fists began to pound on his back.

He didn't pay any attention. She was telling him greater truths with the way her mouth stayed open to him and her own tongue was meshing with his.

Then she gave up that facade. Her hands went to his shoulders. He didn't need his own hands to hold her down anymore. He used them to roam over her body and to feel her firmness. There was a slick patina of sweat over her. But he felt even more wetness when his hands traveled inside her pajamas and he got to her sex. His fingers stroked her body until she gave up all her games of resistance.

It was a matter of pride with Beeker that every woman he was with asked him for it. He never took sex. He never forced himself on any female. Each one had to know that she'd been the one to say "Please."

His fingers were well trained in their maneuvers. They never pressed too hard; they never created pain. They were instruments of pleasure—something that women always found all the more irresistible because the hands belonged to such a large, muscular man. His unexpected gentleness never ceased to attract them.

His mouth moved now as well. His tongue left her mouth, and he caught her lower lip in his jaw. He didn't bite; he only held her vulnerable flesh there. He ran his lips over it even as his teeth held their grip. He was showing off; he wanted her to know just how supple his mouth's movements could be.

She was beginning to thrash underneath him. Her hips were lifting up; her legs spread even farther apart. Her erotic motions, combined with the feel of the silk on his own nearly naked body, were making him want to hurry. But that was always a mistake when you were with a woman you were trying to impress.

Beeker willed himself to slow down. He smiled inside at the thought that this was a military operation. A good soldier always probed the defenses before he attacked.

He let go of her lip, and his mouth—open and wet—moved down her throat, then onto her chest, pushing aside her tunic as it went. He tore open the brassiere with his teeth, holding on to the cloth and tugging until its thin fabric ripped apart and revealed her breasts.

Then it was his tongue again; its tip ran in small swirling motions around the dark circles that outlined her hardening nipples. She was moving faster; her hips were pressing harder; her hands were clutching him more desperately. But she had to surrender first. His hands pushed down the waistband of her pajamas.

"Please," she whispered.

He smiled then. He left her nipple and traveled to her mouth.

He thought he'd worn her out the night before. He also thought he'd worn himself out. But Nur seemed to have something else in mind the next morning. She apparently wanted to even the odds.

He didn't come awake as quickly as usual. It was a soldier's habit to jump up out of bed as soon as his eyes were open. Instead, he seemed to move through some dream stages on his way to consciousness.

The images that floated through his head were all of warm water. He saw himself jumping into a lake back home in Louisiana, naked in the midday sun. Then he was on a beach; the warm sun was heating his flesh, which was still covered with a sheen of sea water.

It took a while for him to realize the source of his dreams. When his eyes opened, he was looking down his own body. There was Nur. He could've fought her off. Maybe, he thought, he should. But it felt wonderful; it was too great a way to start his day.

However, he was, he knew as he came to full awakeness, only a convenience for her. That was all. This was the stud service he'd told himself he'd be performing for her.

When she was finished, she collapsed onto him. The sweat on her breasts and stomach made them stick to each other. He was fully awake now, ready to take her again.

But she was finished with him. She suddenly sat back up and pulled a cord on the side of the bed.

Two female servants quickly answered her summons. She spoke to them in a language he didn't understand. But he certainly understood the tone; the lady was back in control.

"We'll have breakfast here," Nur announced, unashamedly

walking around the room naked. "I've told them to go to your rooms and bring you a change of clothing. Certainly your companions will know what you would choose to wear."

She didn't wait for any answer. Beeker was a little amazed—certainly amused—to see the woman he'd so completely conquered last night act this way, as if a little role reversal in the early morning could wipe out the things she'd said to him in the middle of their nighttime struggle.

He wasn't going to argue. The servants paid no attention to his own nudity. If they weren't going to be worried about it, he wouldn't be, either.

He swung his legs over the side of the bed and stood up. "I'd like a shower," he said.

Nur looked at him; her gaze traveled up and down his body. "Of course." She pointed to a doorway that evidently led to the bathroom. She'd tried to keep the regal tone to her voice, but she'd failed. One little look at him in the right circumstances erased all the effort she'd put into this morning.

Beeker strode across the room with a smile on his face. He was used to losing this battle with Delilah; victory now was sweet.

9

The Patchel family was obviously more comfortable when it didn't have to deal with partygoers. There was less of a possibility that someone would have the bad manners to interrupt their solemnity.

Whatever else was going on with this group, Beeker could see that they weren't out to have a good time. The seriousness was so thick, you could cut the air with it.

It only got worse when the old man came in. Beeker hadn't really had a chance to talk to him or watch him in action last night. Now he saw that the man was crazy. That was the only way to describe it. Billy Leaps stood up with the rest of them when Papa Patchel walked into the room. But Daddy wasn't someone you greeted with a pleasant good morning; that became very obvious.

One by one, his daughter and his three sons went up to him and kissed his hand. "Khalifa," they each said in greeting. He made a gesture that looked like a priest's blessing and then went to his own chair.

His face was masked with a beaming smile. Beeker had seen that smile before, on TV, on the face of an escapee from

Northern California who stared inanely into the camera and told his viewers that they could find eternal happiness if they'd only sell more of his all-natural weight-reduction products to more desperate housewives. That same smile appeared on faces on a lot of the religious programs back home, too. It told you that this guy was very happy that you weren't just as pleased with yourself as he was with himself, and that it was your own fault.

Patchel nodded toward Harry and then Beeker before he sat. The rest of them took their chairs.

"Jamshed—these gentlemen?" The question indicated to his eldest son that he could proceed with the formal introductions. They were done quickly and without handshakes. Foreigners probably didn't get to receive the blessing of the Khalifa, Beeker figured. He almost felt like saying "Aw, shucks," but he stopped himself in time.

"Yes, and you are the gold merchants." Whatever other hustle Papa Patchel might have in mind, there was no question that the man was very happy to talk about yellow ore. But Papa had just as much self-discipline as Beeker. He apparently thought it wasn't appropriate to appear to be a common haggler in the marketplace, not even for one hundred million dollars' worth of bullion. He nodded to Jamshed.

The eldest son wasn't a formidable opponent. He looked weak and had a pronounced belly and spindly arms. His beady eyes were exaggerated by their dark brown color. He was obviously trying to appear tough in front of his daddy, though. He turned to Harry and began his spiel. "It is very propitious for you to arrive at this time with your goods to offer. The size of the transaction is excessive, to say the least. It is most difficult to arrange for that kind of liquidity on such short notice."

Harry'd been prepared for this, of course. He was perfect for the role. His brevity of speech was no handicap here; it just made him appear to be a seasoned negotiator. "I think the amount of the gold deserves a premium on the price. You'd have trouble buying this much at once anywhere else."

That was the cue for them to begin in earnest. Harry sat at the end of the table opposite Papa Patchel and spoke only occasionally, often only to say yes or no to a demand that Jamshed would make.

Beeker watched it all very carefully. Jamshed wasn't a secure man; he kept looking over to Papa to make sure he was doing things right. The middle brother, Lajpat, was more aggressive, too aggressive; he would break in and try to take over the proceedings from Jamshed. He obviously thought he should have the leading role in this. Chandra, the youngest son—in fact, the youngest child; Nur was older than he—treated the entire undertaking as a joke.

At one point the arguing became heated. Nur's nostrils flared, and she jumped into the discussion and angrily told Harry that it was an honor for him to do business with a family like the Patchels and that he should act like it. She had enough sense to pull back a little bit before going over the edge and added that Harry could continue to do extravagant business with the Patchels "later"—whatever that was supposed to mean.

Harry didn't budge.

All through it, Chandra played with a letter opener, stared at his cuticles, studied the wall hangings on the other side of the room, and generally did everything he could to nonverbally communicate what a terrible bore he thought the entire undertaking was.

"Why can't you all simply realize that you're in a stalemate?" Chandra finally said out loud. Everyone stopped speaking and looked at him. "Father"—he turned to look at the head of the table—"in other circumstances would have the leverage to arrange a structured payout to avoid a one-time transfer of money. Mr. Pappathanassiou, on the other hand, might be able to achieve a certain premium for the bulk of his shipment. But it's all negated because you both want the exchange to take place as quickly as possible, each for his own reasons, none of which any of you wants to have investigated. You might as well go for a clean sale based on the London market's close that day. The time difference will make the determination perfectly obvious to everyone."

Papa Patchel looked at his son carefully. The other brothers waited for his response before saying anymore. They weren't used to coming up with original thoughts, and they didn't want to risk one now.

The beatific smile had left Daddy's face during the hassling; now it returned. It hadn't an ounce of sincerity to it, but it relieved the pressure in the room. "Chandra has made a good point. These minute negotiations distract me in any event. The throne mustn't be bothered with the minutiae of the exchequer's problems.

"Jamshed, settle this matter alone, just settle it quickly. Mr. Pappathanassiou will have much to do to arrange the transfer of money and gold." He stood to leave, and the rest of them at the table stood as well. "Make sure that there are five equal exchanges made," Patchel said, dropping the above-it-all air of the emperor and revealing his real understanding of business.

"There should be one each in Bombay, Delhi, Calcutta, Calicut, and Madras, all of equal size, timed two hours apart. As each shipment of gold is handed over, a transfer of money via cable can take place in Switzerland. When we are satisfied with the goods and when Mr. Pappathanassiou is assured that the payments have been made, we can go on to the next step.

"We don't want to tempt common thieves by the presence of so much bullion in one place, do we?" Patchel smiled.

The man was smart, Beeker thought. What he really wanted to make sure of was that Harry didn't pull something on him. Staggering the exchanges made it less possible for a scam to take place.

"Nur," Patchel said, his silly smile back on his face, "I want you to walk with me in the garden."

"Of course, Father." Nur moved to take the offered arm. The pair of them moved out of the room without saying another word.

"Well," Jamshed said, trying to reassert his position as the head of the Patchel negotiators, "there's a certain wisdom to everything the Khalifa has suggested."

Beeker snorted. This kid was going to do it just the way Daddy said it should be done. Did he really think he could gain anything by pulling this bull on them? They could all identify subordination when it was staring them in the face. But not all of them were submissive, Beeker thought as he saw Nur walking with her father outside. Not all of them at all, he told himself as he watched Chandra go back to his studies of his fingernails.

The Patchel family still had some surprises up its sleeves, he bet. He just wondered what they were.

Beeker was swimming in the Olympic-size pool when Nur found him. The pool was the only opportunity for real exercise in the luxurious compound. He'd rather have worked out with weights or taken a couple hours of martial arts practice with Tsali. But there wasn't anything approaching a gymnasium in the place.

The dozens of laps he did in the pool made him feel wonderful. He always felt wonderful whenever he was able to use his body like this. Working, fighting, and physical conditioning were the only things in this world that made sense to Billy Leaps. Other things always intruded in various degrees of pleasure and consternation—like having a son, and being the team leader of the Berets, and women—but he could always go back to basics when he needed to feel in control.

When he finally felt his workout was sufficient, he clung to the edge of the pool with his elbows. He hadn't realized that Nur was there until then. She was sitting on one of the chairs on the patio that surrounded the water. Her legs were crossed. She had a cigarette in her hand; those were omnipresent when her father wasn't around.

Billy hefted his big-muscled frame up onto the ground and got to his feet.

"An attractive picture," Nur said. This was her daytime voice, the one that didn't beg for sex. She wasn't just playacting being in power the way her older brothers were. Beeker sensed that she assumed she'd eventually come to it naturally.

He toweled himself off, rubbing briskly. "I'll be leaving with my partner this afternoon," he began.

"No." Nur stood up and walked over to him. She traced a line from his neck, down the center of his chest, to his navel. "My father has agreed that, given the importance and the size of the transaction we are to accomplish, it will be important that we are all in immediate contact with one another. He's talked to Mr. Pappathanassiou, and they've agreed that you should stay here as a kind of liaison."

Her finger went lower now; it caught on the waistband of his briefs before it rested on the mound of flesh cupped by the swimming suit. "There is important work for you to do here in Agra. We couldn't trust a simple clerk for it, could we?"

She raised her head, and her free hand went to Beeker's neck. She dragged his face down to hers and kissed him.

He jerked himself backward. Damn Harry. This was the shit that Cowboy was good at, not him.

But Nur's hand was pulling him back down again. Her

fingers had spread out, encircling his growing sex. There was no way he could pretend he wasn't interested in this now.

Pretty soon he didn't want to. He maneuvered Nur over to a chaise longue and spread her body over it. Once more, Beeker peeled off his briefs in front of the woman. And once more, there was a hungry look on her face.

10

Beeker kept the horse cantering at a good rate.

Riding across the plains of Hindustan was much more to his liking than the rest of this. The wind gave him welcome relief from the relentless heat of the Indian summer.

His riding clothes were a relief as well. Back home, he'd have disdained jodhpurs as fit only for a wimpy playboy. But here, in the country where they were originally designed, they seemed natural. They clung to his calves and then bloused out at his hips before being cinched at the waist. The khaki material was familiar—the same stuff a tropical-weight uniform would have been constructed of—and it was a welcome change from the formal suits that he was expected to wear at the Patchel mansion.

The horse's mammoth muscles moved between his legs. The speed was exhilarating, and so was the idea of being alone.

Nur was on his mind. He'd learned a lot from watching her and her brothers in action with one another. She was the power; there was no doubt about it. The father was older than Billy Leaps had expected him to be. His children were jockeying for the position of heir. Nur was a manipulative woman. She didn't argue with her male siblings but constantly undercut them, set them against one another so they would waste their time and energy in fraternal battle and leave her dominant on the larger playing field. He'd seen her do this often. It was important information; he knew that. An understanding of internal division was the kind of intelligence you could use against an enemy.

Another horse raced up to join him. Billy Leaps reined in his mount to wait for it. He'd assumed at first that it'd be Nur; she hadn't left him alone very often in the past couple days. But as the rider came closer, he realized it was Chandra, the youngest of the Patchel brothers.

He was the only one who impressed Beeker at all. He was tall and thin, with the dark color of the Indians here. It was similar to Beak's own complexion, but the skin was smoother than that of an American Indian.

The names of the peoples threw Beeker. He was an Indian; he'd been brought up believing that and using that term to describe himself. He was, more specifically, a Cherokee, but that distinction was important only in a few instances. The American society he'd grown up in wasn't interested in his Cherokee nationhood; it wanted a clean racial label for him. Militants these days wanted to call him a Native American. That was fine; that fit. But it would be a long time before that phrase replaced *Indian* in the regular guy's mind.

This man, Chandra Patchel, however, was really an Indian—an inhabitant of India. When the explorers came to the North American continent, they had been looking for this country, this India. That they'd found Beeker's ancestors and mislabeled them was a historical mistake.

That certainly made sense to Billy Leaps—that the arrival of the whites had been a mistake. He suspected that many people here had the same feelings about Europeans.

"Mr. Basalo," Chandra greeted Billy Leaps as he pulled up his mount. They stood facing one another; each of their horses breathed heavily under them. Beeker liked the way Indians talked. English was their main language, although the government was trying to unify the nation with Hindi, a common tongue that it hoped would overcome the divisions that the hundreds of dialects that were spoken on the subcontinent made so obvious. The English that was spoken here had a lilt to it. It was hard to describe; an almost singsong quality infected their speech.

"I'm glad I found you," Chandra went on. "I've been hoping for a moment alone."

"Sure," Beeker said. If the man wanted to talk in private, it could be interesting. But he didn't want to appear obvious. He shook the reins, got his horse moving, and resumed his passage over the plains at a slow walk.

Chandra got his horse to keep pace with Billy Leap's. "You have intrigued me, Mr. Basalo. I don't believe that you are what you appear to be."

Billy Leaps was too well trained to let a remark like that throw him. "What do you mean?"

"You aren't a trader, Mr. Basalo. Perhaps your compatriot is, the Greek. But you don't have the manner of a merchant. You are, instead, like the old warriors in our tales."

"Oh?"

Chandra was content to smile for a while. "You know, with all the troubles that the world is experiencing these days, the soldier of fortune is a very desirable ally." He let that statement float in the air between them. "When empires fall, knights who had been liege to the rulers often become rogues. It's happened often.

"Here, certainly. And in Europe, when the age of chivalry disintegrated, the knights became free-lance, roaming the continent, selling their abilities to whomever would pay the appropriate price. In Japan, also, there were the ronin, the sa-murai who were always a danger to any established authority. The lord who could pay their salaries could amass an army pow-erful enough to challenge the emperor.

"But you know that, Mr. Basalo. You were in Japan recently."

Beeker was glad he was sitting on the rolling muscles of the horse. Its undulating motions covered up the stiffening of his back when Chandra played that ace.

The Berets had been in Japan just months ago. They'd taken out a Russian computer plot that could have ended the high-tech arms race—with the United States as the loser.

Beeker didn't look at Chandra. He didn't want to chance that his eyes would give away anything. He wanted to hear more about the young man's scheme. Was he going to use this infor-mation against Beeker? If so, how?

It suddenly dawned on Billy Leaps that it wasn't surprising that Chandra had found out some things about the Black Berets. It was inevitable, given the actions they'd taken part in over the past few years, that their reputation would be spreading. But how had this guy, this playboy, found himself in channels that shared information about mercenary forces for hire?

"It is usually a new emperor who has a need for ronin, Mr. Basalo." He pronounced Beeker's code name with theatrical emphasis. He wanted to make sure Billy Leaps understood he'd been exposed. "I will be in that market myself, and soon. I'll be paying premiums for those services—higher ones than my father will pay for your Greek's gold."

"Higher than your sister?" Beeker played his own trump.

"I am sure that my beloved sister requires certain services that are of no interest to me, for which she will compensate you," Chandra joked. "But there are others—less personal, shall we say?—for which I will gladly outbid her."

"What is it you want?" Let's get on with it, Beeker thought. There's no reason to play this charade out. He pulled in his horse's reins, and this time he turned to stare directly at Chandra.

The young Brahmin was just as serious. "Must we continue to play games about your identity?"

"I'll tell you something, Chandra. If you were smart, you'd be happy I have a code name. Things are cleaner this way. Sometimes it doesn't pay to know much about trivial details."

"A man's identity is trivial?"

"When all you want is the man's gun—yeah, it is."

Chandra nodded. "What do you know about my family? About their plans?"

"They want a lot of gold. They're rich enough to buy it. What else is there to know?"

"That my father believes he's the descendant of the Mogul emperors."

"I've heard the talk."

Chandra hesitated for a brief moment. He was at a decision point: Would he trust this man further? But he needed to show off a bit of his own knowledge, to let Beeker know they were equal in this bargaining.

"You did great damage to a Swedish arms trader in Japan. My father doesn't yet realize that it was you who interfered with one of his most beloved schemes, the one he actually thought would lead to a monarchy here in India."

Beeker didn't take the bait. The "great damage" he'd done was actually permanent damage; the man was dead.

"You may actually have forced him to go much further than he would have before. My father is about to destroy India."

Chandra waited for a response. Beeker didn't give one to him.

"You Americans have fallen into the same trap in some of your quests for power. I remember the infamous film clip in which an American officer explained to the camera why a Vietnamese village had just been totally destroyed. It was, he claimed, to save it from falling to the Communists.

"My father and my sister are willing to destroy India for the sake of having it—or what's left of it. I don't think you want that to happen. I know I don't. I think you're here to stop them. I want to help."

"You said you didn't trust a man who wouldn't tell you his name. But you want me to trust one who'd do in his family."

"Do you know how my father amassed his fortune? Or how his father and grandfather before him did the same? They were all Brahmins, members of the highest class. The caste laws forbid them to take part in commerce. You've heard my sister disdain tradesmen, I'm sure. That's at the root of her feelings.

"But you can also certainly see that the Patchels have a great deal of money, a fortune many times over. How did they achieve it? By marriage—marriage to daughters of the hated merchants.

"In their quest for prestige, some of the richest men in India have foolishly married their daughters to Patchel men. A smart Brahmin man like my father, seeking fortunes, will take many wives in succession. My father, as old as he is, would happily take a new one now.

"He can, you see, because his last wife, my mother, died recently. Her death was of suspicious circumstances. I loved my mother. I'll have my revenge.

"There's more, I don't doubt it. I learned much from her; I learned how to appear stupid when I am actually very smart. It disarms one's opponents. I've also accepted her background, not my father's, as my own heritage, more than any one knows. I have no desire to defend an antiquated caste system. I'd rather take the Patchel family resources and create a commercial empire than a military one.

"But to accomplish that I need the family money. I also need to have a country in which to trade and invest securely. If my father and sister succeed, I'll have neither. I was preparing ways to thwart my family's plans before you arrived on the scene. But now that you are here, I think I will cast my lot with you."

"What is your family up to?" Beeker knew there was no more reason to play games. Chandra had made some interesting points, and he was potentially an ally. "You say they're opposed to commerce. But I saw their factories on the outskirts of the city."

"Those!" Chandra laughed. "Yes. I can see I'll have to show you more. But we have to return to the modern age, friend. Let's take the horses back to their stable. I'll show you some things I know you'll be interested in."

For the first few minutes that Beeker was in the passenger seat of the Mercedes 560-SL, he thought he'd overestimated Chandra terribly. The guy was just a hotshot trying to show off, he thought now. He was driving the Mercedes as if he thought Beeker would be impressed that he knew how to slam his foot down on the accelerator.

But when they took the first corner, Billy Leaps changed his mind and realized that Chandra was something else entirely. He maneuvered the speedster with all the skill of a Monte Carlo veteran.

That was the key to the guy, Beeker realized: He led you to think he was a playboy. The cars were fast and glitzy, and the mind seem facile—but that was only superficial.

Beeker relaxed against the bucket seat. Now that he knew he was in capable hands, he could sit back and enjoy the ride. His pleasure was increased by the admiration he felt for the man's skill.

The Mercedes pulled up in front of one of the huge buildings in the Patchel complex, on the outskirts of Agra. A guard came running up to them. "Mr. Patchel"—he was obviously overwhelmed at having a member of the ruling family in his compound and upset at which one it was—"you are not—"

"Get out of my way," Chandra said imperiously. "I'm here to show my sister Nur's new bodyguard around."

The mention of the woman's name changed the tone of the guard's speech and the complexion of his skin. "If you say so, Mr. Patchel."

"I do." Chandra was back in his role as dilettante. Something of the conspirator in him had been revealed back when they were on horseback, alone on the plains. But now, Beeker realized, Chandra behaved as if he were trying out for a bit part in a bad movie about gay bars.

Beeker could see that the guard thought the same thing. As soon as Chandra strode by him, he sneered openly at the effeminate manner in which the Patchel brother walked.

Billy Leaps followed Chandra through the doors of the huge industrial building. The signs announced that this was the warehouse of the Patchel Bicycle Plant. Beeker had believed that when he read it; bicycles were a vital part of the transportation network in India. A good businessman would invest in their manufacture.

But once they were inside, he was surprised. "But I've seen the workers entering and leaving every morning," Beeker said out loud.

"Yes, friend. But for shifts of what?" Chandra teased.

Spread out inside the structure were rows of Messerschmitt BO-105Ps, the deadly armed helicopters that were the backbone of the West German Luftwaffe. Against the walls, in military precision that even Beeker had to admire, were stacked lines of Karlsrupa machine guns. "How did they get them?" Beeker couldn't help asking out loud. "They're Swedish. When it comes to the arms trade, the Swedes' assholes are so tight, a strawberry seed couldn't get past them."

"We are a neutral country, friend," Chandra said. "Don't you remember? India is one of the few states with whom all the arms manufacturers in the world will do business.

"As to those workers—they are my father's private army. They come here for their training."

"Armed like this?" Beeker asked in a state of awe.

"I think, if we are to do any more business, that we must go and have a long talk. I think, if you are interested in what I propose, that we will have to put our cards on the table with one another.

"You know"—Chandra was leading Beeker out the door—"I spend a great deal of time in Europe. I enjoy the life there, away from my family. It becomes difficult to hide how much I loathe them all. The act is wearying.

"In France, on the Côte d'Azur, I met an incredibly beautiful woman. She was blonde—so blonde, one assumed at first that she had dyed her hair. Then when one got to know her, one knew that it was natural, as natural as her breasts."

Beeker pulled his arm out of Chandra's grasp. He turned to the Indian ready for a fight.

"I don't think America's most famous mercenary needs to resort to violence when confronted with a playboy, Mr. Beeker."

Billy Leaps stood there. This man was smart—and dangerous. He'd pulled Beak through the whole thing knowing perfectly well who he was, not just suspecting it.

"We would do much better to talk openly with one another," Chandra said. His face was shrewd now. "The time for playing poker with each other is past. India is in danger, Mr. Beeker. If you save it, I will become a rich man. If you don't, we will both die."

11

"It'd be a bitch to blow up." Marty Appelbaum was standing at the end of the reflecting pool and studying the objective. "I mean, all those minarets or whatever it is you call them. They'd be hell. They'd just shatter and send shrapnel flying all over the damned place."

He shook his head solemnly like the professional he was when faced with a difficult problem. "I just don't know. It'd be real messy."

Every once in a while, Roosevelt Boone had to remember who he was dealing with. This was one of the times when he'd forgotten. But you just couldn't let that slip from your mind, because if you did, it hit you blind-sided. "For Christ's sake, Marty! That's the fucking Taj Mahal!"

"Well, I don't care if it's Grant's Tomb, it'd still be a bitch to blow up!" The little blond man was getting defensive. "Isn't that why I'm here—to blow things up? Isn't that my job?" He had his hands on his hips and had turned to confront the huge black man whose bulk was nearly twice his own.

"Marty." Rosie spoke in a very slow and deliberate tone

now. "You are not here in Agra to blow up the Taj Mahal. I don't know why you are here. I don't know why I'm here. But I promise you, we are not going to destroy one of the great monuments of world architecture."

"Well, that's good." Marty backed down a bit. "Like I say, it'd be messy. You want a good solid building for a pretty explosion, one that you can trust structurally. All that showy stuff they have on there, those little pieces of decoration they plastered onto the main building—it'd just be hell if you got a bomb going. I mean, it'd all just turn into a lot of small missiles. It's marble, isn't it? That's some of the worst. I tell you, Rosie, that stuff just shatters, and then you've got real problems the way the small pieces fly at you.

"There was this building once in St. Louis that they hired me to do in. They had these strange statues all around the top floor, statues of monsters and ghouls—"

"Gargoyles, Marty. They were gargoyles."

"Goy girls?" Marty laughed that sickeningly shrill laugh of his. "Man, Rosie, those were some ugly goyische females, then!" He was always trying to come up with a joke that would allow him to think he was really part of the team. Then he'd work it to death.

Rosie reminded himself that Marty really only just wanted to be one of them. It was a disadvantage, he told himself, that the guy worked under this constant insecurity. He was like some poor guy with crutches—you had to try to avoid thinking of his problems. You shouldn't focus on them; you should think of the good things about the person.

But Rosie was damned if he could think of a single thing that redeemed Marty Appelbaum as a human being. There was not one. The laugh that cut through the air now was sharp enough to slice a hole in you. The man's face was the pastiest white of any Caucasian face that Rosie had ever seen. His eyes were always runny, even here in this place that was nearly a desert. His body reminded Rosie of a chicken's, it was so scrawny.

Why did he have to put up with this sorry excuse for a living person?

"I tell you, though, I'd be willing to try it if it had to be done." Marty was back to a serious tone of voice. "It'd be hard, you know that. But if anyone can do it, I can!"

And that was the answer. Rosie looked at the grandeur of the Taj Mahal, and he realized that if there were a clean and efficient way to destroy it, Appelbaum would be the one to do the job. The man loved bombs; he loved them the way Rosie loved the sweet taste between a woman's thighs. TNT was Marty's sugar, Rosie realized. And that's why he—and all the rest of them—put up with the guy.

It was just as well that Cowboy and Harry weren't here to listen to the little blond man's crap, though. They would've blown up. This was a monument to a man's love for his wife. The Shah Jahan had built the Taj Mahal in the seventeenth century to display the immortal grief he had felt when his bride, the beautiful Mumtaz Mahal, died. This was the physical expression of what Harry felt all the time, living without the woman he loved.

Harry would revere this place more than any other building on earth. If he had heard Appelbaum talk about blowing it to smithereens, he'd be the one to turn into a human volcano.

'Course, nowadays Cowboy wasn't much better. After what had happened to that Portuguese skirt of his down in Goa, you'd think Cowboy and Harry were ready to join a goddamned monastery together and devote their lives to the memories of their vestal virgins or some such shit.

And these were the men he was supposed to fight with—a bunch of grunts who'd lost half their brains and most of their souls in Vietnam. Which was better: The huge Greek running around thinking every woman he met deserved a pedestal? Cowboy wanting to marry all the ones he found? Marty—who never did seem to find a woman—wanting to play pick-up sticks with one of the wonders of the world? Beeker, the half-breed, half-assed ex-Marine, wishing he'd been consigned to be a boot at Parris Island for the rest of his life?

Some days Rosie just wanted out. On those days he wished he were back in the basement of Newark General Hospital peeling off cadavers' skin for bandages, whistling tunes, and watching the color of their blood as it poured out of the dead veins, nearly coagulated.

Rosie laughed out loud at himself. There he was, worried about their sanity, and he was daydreaming about going back to *that*.

Sometimes, he realized, a man has to understand that he gets just the companions he deserves. He put one of his heavily muscled arms around Marty's bony shoulder and hugged him a bit. "Come with me, my man. We got to meet up with our folks at that hotel soon. But we got time to elbow up to a bar and throw a few down our throats 'fore they get there, don't we?"

Marty looked up at Rosie with the on-guard look of a playground whipping boy who mistrusts the school bully's sudden, uncharacteristic friendliness. But then he let his fear disappear into his omnipresent hope that he might really make it as one of the gang after all.

"Sure, Rosie, my man. Let me buy for you."

He did it all wrong, of course. Appelbaum was doomed always to say the wrong thing in the wrong way. But Rosie wasn't concerned about it now. Right now, they were the walking wounded of the world together. That was all there was to it. They were in it together, and this was no time to try to change the cast of characters in your life.

At least, it wasn't as if Rosie's guesses were about what kind of trouble they might be in now were at all right. If anything, he figured, things were worse than he suspected.

He should be scared. He should be concerned. But he only laughed. Why bother with those problems when he had the world's greatest mad bomber right there under his own wing?

Rosie laughed all the way back to the hotel.

"Where's Beeker, Harry?" Rosie asked when the Greek showed up at their hotel room with Tsali but not with the leader of the Black Berets.

"Bad stuff," Harry answered. Rosie took a deep breath and willed himself not to lose his temper. The Greek was notorious for his short answers to questions, responses that seldom presented anything more than the bare bones of the required information.

What a group this was getting to be, Rosie thought all over again. "I know it must be bad, Harry, because when I look outside the window, I do not see the fields of our farm back in Louisiana," Rosie said softly. "If it wasn't bad, I'd be home drinkin' beer, eatin' pigs' feet, and fuckin' sweet, ripe women. I am not doin' any of those things. Therefore, things are bad."

"You got it, Rosie."

Hold on to your temper. These are the men you honor and love above all others. These are the best fighting men in the world. Do not have a screaming fit. Rosie willed himself to unclench his fists.

"Let's talk specifics, Harry. About just what is bad and in just what way it is."

"Well, there's the father, that's one. He thinks he's some kinda guru. Thinks he's God's messenger on earth, or maybe it's that he thinks he's God."

"Uh-huh," Rosie coaxed, wanting more.

"Well, he started the whole thing. Those killings all over India—"

Cowboy's head jerked up. "Carmelita?"

"Probably, but not specifically her. I mean, he didn't tell someone to go out and off her, you know? He just put it into all these people's heads that India was being polluted by Westerners and that the poisoned parts had to be cleansed.

"That's how it goes, isn't it?" Harry turned, to Tsali who nodded agreement.

Harry turned back to the other men. "It's called the Din Illahi, this religion of his. It's getting them all hot and bothered, all of them—the Sikhs, the Hindus, the Moslems, all of them. They're beginning to think it's the real Indian religion, see?

"So, Papa Patchel, he's bringing the whole thing above ground. He's starting this thing that'd be like a religious crusade back in the States. He's going around and preaching to crowds and all of it, proclaiming the new word, that kind of stuff. He's beginning in Calcutta. Then he's going to Delhi, and on and on."

"Uh-huh." Rosie didn't dare smile, even though these were more words than he'd heard Harry speak at one time in years. "What's wrong with that?"

"Well, he's saying that there's all this pollution, like I told you. It's in the women—that's why those guys went after your Carmelita girl, Cowboy. She was defiled by your 'seed,' they said."

Marty started to giggle, but one dark look from Cowboy shut him up.

"He's saying it's the same as Bhopal. That it's the same thing, this poisoning. And he's gonna tell them that there's another, bigger one coming up."

"And he's going to make sure it's very big." Rosie finished the thought for him. "Like nuclear-bomb big."

"Gonna do it in Calcutta and then Bombay, the both of

them. And he's got these troops that are gonna set off a religious war like you wouldn't believe, all at once. Gonna send some of them to Amritsar and dress them so they look like Hindus attacking the Golden Temple, the Sikh religious place. Then he's got others; they'll dress like Moslems, and they're gonna throw dead cows into the Ganges, which the Hindus think is sacred. Then he's gonna have some of those men of his attack some mosques.

"It goes on. You wouldn't believe it, it just goes on. By the time the man's through, there won't be much left of India."

"And he's going to take his army and march it around and make himself king?"

"Hell, no," Harry said. "All his army's gonna do is secure an area around here, around Agra, about the size of Louisiana. Then he's gonna let the rest of the country go to hell and high water. He's not gonna do the conquering. He's just gonna be the only stable force in the country. He's gonna wait until, city by city, state by state, they come to him.

"That's why he wants the gold: to show them his wealth. No other money in India will be worth shit then. But the gold will convince them all that they're on the side of the winner.

"With enough gold—the hundred million we're supposed to supply, along with the rest he's hoarded—he can buy anything left that'd be worth buying in India, and *anybody* worth buying, too."

"But the Russians! The Chinese! They're just waiting to walk across the border and finally take this damned place."

"Beeker figured that out," Harry explained. "The United States and the Russians and the Chinese—none of them's ever gonna let the other one get across the border. It'd be the end, Rosie. If we let either of the Communist countries take India, they'd have won the lottery. They'd be too big, they'd have too many people, they'd control too much.

"So this Papa Patchel, he figures they're just gonna stand each other off. And the Indians won't want any of them by the time he's through."

"How can he be so sure?"

"Because of the bombs. He's gonna blame that on the Russians. He's gonna blow another chemical plant, just like Bhopal, and that he'll blame on us. The Chinese he's gonna pull in some other way. By the time he's done, no Indian will want anything to do with anyone who's a foreigner at all."

"And we got to stop it?"

And you must be the leader. My father says so. He will join you later. But you must take charge. Tsali signed that message to Rosie.

The big black man shook his head with renewed disgust as he looked around the room one more time. "It ain't going to be easy."

12

So this is what we're up against.

Rosie stood at the back of the huge amphitheater in Calcutta. The whole thing was reminiscent of a revival meeting back home. He recognized a lot of what was going on. This was a guru, he realized, who'd carefully learned his lessons from Americans.

There were the clean-looking, pleasant young pages, smiling with delight in a way that you didn't often see in a city as destitute as Calcutta.

These kids weren't slowly dying of starvation and disease on the city's streets. They may have been happy because they'd found God, but they were probably really this happy just 'cause they'd been eating regularly.

But the point was the impression they made on the older people—Rosie knew that. And that impression was good. In fact, it was downright wholesome. After the incredible pushing, shoving crowds of Calcutta, in which adolescents intent on hustling whatever they could elbowed their way past old ladies and stepped on old men's feet, here were bright smiles of obedience and discipline.

Their clothes were clean. Their eyes were bright. Their smiles were dazzling—just like the fundies did at home. There was even music, warming people up. It wasn't the rousing spirituals that Rosie'd heard in his youth; instead, this was traditional music. But that was part of the message, he knew, a reminder of the glory of ancient India. The sitars weren't trying to sound like a new wave of rock 'n' roll. They were evoking images from the past, of the might of the Moguls and of the destiny of an empire before it'd been thwarted by the British.

All this careful orchestration had still another dimension that was crucially different from anything that went on in the States, though. Rosie was impressed by it, all right; he was very impressed by the staging. Because this wasn't going to be just some preacher who walked out onto the platform. This was going to be an emperor, one who just might be God.

There wasn't a lectern; there was a throne. Above it rose a canopy that Rosie bet was real gold. In fact, there were so many armed guards that he was sure it was gold. No man, not even a god, needed that many guards. But there were dozens of guards, each ostentatiously holding a machine gun, spread around the place where the man would sit.

Someone came out onto the stage, and a hush fell over the crowd. This was the one who'd warm them up, Rosie figured. He spoke in awed tones, telling the people to prepare themselves for the sight of the Khalifa.

Some of the guards moved quickly and lit huge oil lamps on either side of the throne. They were symbolic, the audience was told, of the *hom*, the fire sacrifice that was demanded of the god of the Din Illahi. That would come, they were promised, when the time was right, when the Khalifa determined that India was ready for the final cleansing.

Then he came on. Rosie had always thought that in person,

ministers in revivals were never even close to being as potent looking as their press said they were. They had always fallen short of his expectations when he was a kid. But he had to hand it to this dude. The man looked like a king. He was even wearing a crown, made of gold like the throne.

The unarmed men on the stage fell to the floor, performing the *sijdah*, the prostration he'd seen Moslems perform in their prayers to Allah. This emperor wasn't going to be satisfied with a casual greeting when his rule came, that was for sure.

Some of the people in the audience tried to imitate the *sijdah*, but the aisles were too narrow. Still, the way they reacted showed Rosie just how powerful the appeal of this man's message was. They didn't give up simply because they couldn't perform the gesture of subservience. They cried out in frustration. All around him, people pushed to get to the walkways between the sections of the amphitheater where there was room for the *sijdah*.

These people were hungry for it, Rosie realized. They'd fought each other for centuries. They'd been humiliated by dozens of other nations, many of them with fewer people and resources. They were still shrugging of the remnants of the colonialism that had insinuated itself into their lives. They wanted glory, and they wanted a leader and a message that would unite them.

The Khalifa was offering them the Din Illahi, and they could all buy into it. It was, he told them, the religion that had made India great centuries before. It was the force that had united them. It had brought them glory and awe in the world. It could work again.

He would lead them.

Rosie felt his skin crawl with the subtext of the message that he was hearing. Inevitably, there was a hint of the superiority of believers over all others. That hint could grow to become the justification for killing nonbelievers; it certainly had in other places. There was the militant nationalism that had led to the destruction of so many other governments. There was the beginnings of a call for the holy war. Under the calm words he was hearing, Rosie heard the unmistakable cry of hatred for others.

Now he understood how dangerous this man was.

He moved to leave the amphitheater. He didn't want to know any more. He understood at gut level that this was going to be his. He knew instinctively that he would stop Patchel from becoming the Khalifa of the Din Illahi.

If he didn't, he also knew the whole thing was over.

"What a fucked-up assignment," Marty Appelbaum griped.

"Just figure it out, will you?" Harry asked. He tried to keep exasperation out of his voice. Marty had enough trouble with the rest of the guys. Harry was always trying to help him by acting like he was the man's friend. He wasn't, not really, but he tried to make believe it was true. Everyone needed a friend in the world.

"Well, I think it's a fucked-up waste of my time and energy."

They were standing on a small hill overlooking a vast chemical complex in the Deccan, the southern half of India, by International Medicinals. The name of the corporation was misleading; it hadn't produced a medicine in decades. With its knowledge of chemistry, it had transformed itself into one of the largest plastics manufacturers in the world. As by-products of the petrochemical process, it also made many other high-tech products.

But they weren't the kind used in any doctor's office. They were the kind for exterminating insects, defoliating forests, and cleaning jet aircraft engines. They were the most lethal compounds man had ever created.

"Look, I'm sorry you can't blow it up," Harry finally conceded. "But it's just not part of the plan. What we have to do is make sure someone else doesn't blow it up."

"I feel like a traitor to my profession." Marty was downcast. He really thought it was unfair that he wasn't doing any demolition. "Do you think," he asked softly, "there's any chance Beeker will give me that building in Agra to make up for this?"

"No, Marty, no. We've told you over and over again—it's a precious masterpiece. You can't blow it up."

"Damn. It'd be a real challenge, making sure it imploded, fell in on itself. I'd make sure the marble didn't hurt anyone. I was just thinking out loud when I told Rosie it'd be dangerous."

"No, Marty. What you have to do is study this plant and figure out how someone else would blow it up. Then you have to stop him."

"But I don't know his mind. I can't assume he'd approach it like I would. I'm a demolition expert! What if it's a rank amateur? He'd probably try to do all kinds of asshole things to the place that I wouldn't even consider. You're asking Michelangelo to anticipate how a kindergarten kid would fingerpaint!"

"Go back to your beginnings, Marty. Think how you would have done it years ago."

"Shit!" Marty kicked his feet into the Deccan earth. "I'll figure it out. But alone? Damn, can't you at least stay with me, Harry? I don't want to do this alone."

"Marty, you know I have to be in Bombay for the first transfer of the gold. Rosie's sticking with Papa Patchel. Tsali and Beeker are back at the headquarters. And Cowboy's got his own assignment."

Marty sighed deeply. "I'll do it. Somehow I'll figure out how this fool's going to get in there."

Cowboy stood in the middle of the Indian Air Force base near Delhi. Delilah walked up to him. He nodded. That was all the greeting he was going to give her.

"I have a bird for you," she said.

"I suspected that was why I'm here," he responded sarcastically.

She didn't take the bait but continued talking evenly, as she always did. "It's not been easy. India isn't actually one of our allies. They cling to their neutrality. But I've convinced them that you're a special mechanic on assignment from the manufacturer and that you're only coincidentally American. They've bought the new Lynx from Britain. Can you fly it?"

It would have been silly to wonder why, if the Indians were so suspicious of his being American, they had accepted her as an authoritative source.

He looked at the Lynx and knew it'd do just fine. He didn't even bother to respond to her stupid question. It was a matter of pride for him that he could pilot anything that had ever been made. The most it ever took was a half-hour with a manual and five minutes for a look-see around a cockpit.

She got the message. "This way."

They walked down the runway to a squat-looking machine. At least, it would have looked like that to anyone else, but to Cowboy the potential was immediately obvious.

"Westland's the manufacturer. They've redesigned the Lynx to be a dedicated armed helicopter," Delilah began. The model they were looking at was the Lynx 3. Cowboy knew they were becoming the backbone of the British helicopter offensive force. The bird could never take on the Hinds or the Huey Cobras that'd been the major part of the U.S. Air Force in Vietnam. But it would do this job.

He listened vaguely as she went through her rap about TOW missiles and the 40-millimeter grenade launchers. He looked inside the cockpit while she talked and immediately sensed which controls worked which ways.

"It's smaller than I like."

"I can't do better."

"It's a bird," he said. "That's what's important."

"What's important is that arsenal they've built up. If they get any of those Messerschmitts in the air before you destroy them on the ground, you won't have much of a chance."

"What do you mean?" he asked angrily.

"Cowboy, the Indian Air Force doesn't have anything to compare to the Messerschmitts."

"You're right. But the Patchels don't have anything to compare to *me*."

She lifted an eyebrow. "I've never doubted that, Cowboy. I only want you to have the resources you need."

"They're all here, Delilah."

He made himself appear to be busy. He'd meant what he said. But there was a difference in his attitude this time. He was going to do the job, but he wasn't sure he was going to come back from the mission. The truth was, he didn't know if he wanted to.

He'd been fighting all his adult life, except for the few years that he'd been smuggling, years he barely remembered through his cocained memory. They didn't count. It was getting so that not much did count.

The woman . . .

What they didn't understand about Cowboy was that she'd been killed just when he wanted to marry her. They only thought of him as leaving his wives after his marriages. They recalled only his feelings and emotions when he was trying to get away from one of his wives.

But this was different. Someone had murdered his Carmelita before her time at the altar with him. She was—and would be for a long time—his beloved. He'd been hurt, hurt much more badly than they knew.

That meant he wanted revenge. For once, Cowboy cared about a mission. He cared about it so badly that he didn't mind if he died.

He sat at the controls. His fantasies weren't about blowing up the arsenal at the Patchels'. He was dreaming about killing Papa Patchel himself. He was fantasizing about this Lynx diving down onto the human god as he sat on the golden throne Rosie'd talked about, and in his dream the Lynx was firing off grenades, aiming them right for Patchel himself.

They didn't know that about him. They'd made a major miscalculation. For once, Billy Leaps Beeker had misjudged who he was working with.

Cowboy felt sweat building up, the tensions he felt were horrible. He looked over at Delilah. She was talking to some Indian officer and didn't see his look—the look of a desperate man. Maybe she would have done something if she had seen it. But by the time she returned, the expression was different. All she saw was determination, and that was something she always expected to see on the face of a Black Beret.

13

Patchel's movement was gaining ground every day. Beeker read the papers, and he could see the handwriting on the wall. It was like every other time that a dictator succeeded in taking over a country.

First, the press stopped making fun of him. The derisive cartoons that used to appear were gone. There were still strident calls for resistance from the socialist press, but they were a lonely voice in the crowd.

Various religious leaders were making moves to accommodate Patchel. They were trying to induct him into their private circle, hoping he'd be happy being one of the accepted members.

The government was beginning to try to do the same thing. The Prime Minister made a visit to the self-proclaimed Khalifa and talked to him. Not to be outdone, the opposition parties sent delegations, too.

Patchel had worked for months to set the stage for exactly this. He wasn't going to be bought off by symbolic gestures; his conceit was too strong. Beeker had seen that at that first meeting. Any father who would have his own children kiss his hand in homage was over the hill, into the territory of grand self-delusions. He actually believed all his own propaganda. That would make him all the more dangerous.

Everyone had either ignored him or underestimated the appeal of a nationally binding religious and political movement. Now Patchel's attraction was becoming overwhelmingly obvious.

There were rumors of fire sacrifice. The *hom* was being honored as part of the Din Illahi. For now, it was only animals. But the bloodthirst of the masses was being raised to a fever pitch. Reports were circulating of true believers throwing themselves onto the fires in fits of religious fervor.

In Agra the existence of the private army was becoming less and less secret. The soldiers were wearing their uniforms on the street—something they'd never done before. But Patchel and his sons weren't foolish, Beeker saw. They'd ordered everyone back into civilian clothes as soon as they learned what was going on. The enormous cache of arms had to remain a secret. The Patchels didn't want the Indian Army to be alerted too quickly.

But the word got out. The government didn't dare act decisively; there was an inexplicable outbreak of Sikh-Hindu violence in the Punjab, and there were rumors of troop movements in Pakistan. The army was deployed to meet those more obvious and pressing threats. There were more converts then, not the believing kind but the kind that thought they'd better be on the right side. They were the ones betting that Patchel could win.

The tide of his movement swept relentlessly over India. His personal crusade was the force behind it. He threw all his remaining money and all his energy into it. The size of the crowds increased at each stop. It would end soon, here in Agra, the ultimate stop. A small coliseum in the city was being renovated in his honor. It was being reconstructed with a special section for the international media.

Patchel was no longer a fluke, another interesting, if harmless, Indian religious leader. He was a political—and potentially military—force to be reckoned with.

Beeker watched all this happen from the Patchel mansion. He was under surveillance at all times, so obviously that he wondered if the entire operation had been uncovered. But then he understood that the surveillance was only because he was Nur's constant bedmate.

The frustration grew inside of him. This wasn't the role he was used to being in. He wanted to be in the field. But he couldn't act differently. He had the best way of all to learn the Patchel's plans: His head was on the pillow of the crown princess of the renewed dynasty.

Nor dared he cause alarm by leaving. He had to maintain the facade of being the kept man—him! Billy Leaps Beeker, the stud-in-residence here at the mansion!

Not for long, he thought every time Nur made another move on him. Their lovemaking was becoming more passionate; he now came close to violence when he took her. She misunderstood all that. She thought it was proof of her attractiveness. The fool didn't realize that he was acting out his fury in the bed they shared.

She'd find out the truth soon enough.

No one would have expected a man like Roosevelt Boone to be so good at undercover work. They'd think that Rosie would be unable to change his appearance. He was a six-foot-two-inch-tall, heavily muscled black man. He wasn't the kind that blended into the background.

Yet people didn't really see blacks, even here in India with its own dark-skinned people. They saw images of blacks; that was all. Just the way they assumed that Tsali's inability to hear indicated total disablement, they looked for only the most sur-face of indications of who Rosie was. He'd always used this against his enemies.

He was becoming obsessed with Papa Patchel. He went to every one of the man's revivals. He went in a different costume each time. In Delhi, where he wore a suit and tie with a crisp white shirt, it was assumed that he was an African diplomat. In Bombay, wearing an open shirt and a series of ostentatious gold chains hanging over his bare chest, someone asked if he was an American rock star.

If you lined up all the people who saw Rosie in each of those cities and asked if he was the same man, they'd all tell you it was impossible. That was because they hadn't viewed an individual, they'd seen a stereotype. The stereotype was what'd stuck in their minds.

So he was able to trail Patchel without arousing even the notice of the machine-gun-wielding bodyguards. He could smile at the same one and show the same big white teeth, and the se-curity person would just look right through him.

That's what let Rosie know that there was a routine to the whole thing. Patchel held meetings all day. He activated the re-gional people and brought them up to date. He also held court for the new "converts" who were desperate to make sure that they hadn't missed out on the train. These confabs were strictly limited to those who could get by the awesome guards.

Then there were the evenings, when Patchel would hold his outdoor rallies. They were more and more crowded with every stop as the common people gathered to see the man who would deliver India into greatness. They would throw themselves to the ground in the *sijdah*. They were desperate to believe now. They wanted deliverance, and Patchel was their best hope since Gandhi.

As he watched the leader at work in Bombay, Rosie knew he'd

have to take Patchel out either during one of the revivals or else immediately before or after. He was in touch with Delilah. He knew what he needed to do the job. She'd have to get it for him.

"All praise the Khalifa of the Din Illahi!" the crowd roared in approval as Rosie watched. "All praise the savior of India!" The cheering surged to new heights.

And Rosie watched as the Khalifa came onstage—except he saw the man differently from anyone else. When he looked at Patchel these days, Rosie saw him as if through the cross hairs of a gunsight. He was game for the Black Berets now. That was all.

Patchel had become the object of Cowboy's interest, too. And Cowboy's attention was just as dangerous for the superguru as Rosie's.

The flier was being consumed by a fiery obsession about Patchel. He was the murderer of Carmelita. Cowboy's personal vendetta against him was utterly private. That was its greatest danger. He had instinctively moved into the secret world of the compulsive. Everyone around him was his enemy. Everyone was somehow trying to stop him from achieving the one goal that was of paramount importance to him.

He still had moments of objectivity, when he'd remember that he was a Black Beret and had obligations to the rest of the team. He'd try to hang on to those. They were, he sometimes understood, his links to sanity. But they would soon slip out of his grasp.

He was in a strange reality. It was like nothing he'd experienced since he took psychedelic drugs years ago. He would drift in and out of various states of mind. Some of them were fine; others were insane. But he was losing touch with the border between them.

Every time he got behind the controls of the Lynx 3, he

had to struggle to stop himself from simply going to where he knew or thought Patchel was right then and blowing the fucker out of the modern age.

Why was he one of the Berets, anyway? he wondered. What difference did it make? Why had they bothered to get back together again after Nam? There was no good reason; there was no real cause. They could be individual people, couldn't they? Couldn't they go after their own things by themselves?

Without knowing it, Cowboy was answering his own nagging questions—because he was proof of why they *had* to be together. The way his mind was disintegrating was the reason they clung to one another and to Beeker. Together, they could act with rational coordination and support. Alone, they would each fall apart, fall into isolation, and become uncontrolled killing machines, the way they'd been taught to be in Nam.

Cowboy would become a time bomb the moment he gave up his last tie to the group. Without them, he would be a loose cannon in the world.

But they didn't know about it. They couldn't have seen it happen. He treated them like enemies or officers from whom his real feelings had to be hidden.

Between sessions with the Lynx, he kept busy flying a Learjet around India. Marty kept needing things special-delivered from Delilah. Harry was working out a way to fool the Patchels into believing that they were really going to get all that gold. Delilah insisted on touching base with every one of them. The worry she displayed was new for her, an emotion Cowboy'd never seen before on her.

As long as he kept busy and as long as there was reason to be in touch with them, he could hold on. The rest of the time, when he was alone, he contemplated the power he held in the grenades of the Lynx and the rest of it took over him.

When he was in the Lynx, flying over one or another Indian Air Force base, it would come out. He was losing track of which place he was flying from. The credentials Delilah had secured gave him unlimited access for the next two weeks. He was utterly mobile and could get his hands on a Lynx 3 in any part of the country he wanted to.

He'd be manipulating the controls and studying the armaments on the bird; it would all be registering in his head—but in the cold, calculating way of a computer lodged in a human body.

All of him that was human was consumed with the image of Patchel and with the only other image that mattered to him: *Carmelita . . . Carmelita . . . Carmelita.*

14

Tsali watched Delilah move around their hotel suite in Delhi. She was deep in thought, the way his father was when a crisis was upon them. He paid attention to that. He trusted this woman. She had been kind to him, and she had become important to him. Her being this concerned meant as much to him as his father displaying the same worriedness.

She sat down in a chair opposite him and then only suddenly remembered that he was there. Coming from her, that was another indication of how serious matters were becoming.

She reached over and took his hand in hers. It was a subtle gesture, a soft one, the kind of thing she did so well. It carried a lot with it. It told him she hadn't really forgotten him; it let him know that he was part of whatever was going on; it said he was important in whatever the solution was going to be.

"They aren't meant to act this way, Tsali. None of them is prepared to operate solo. Damn! This country is so huge, though! And Patchel is so powerful and devious! How else could we have gone about it?"

There was no answer—they both knew that. He read her

lips but didn't bother to try to respond to her question.

He didn't hear the knock on the door, but he knew from the way she reacted that there'd been one. It happened to all the hearing people he'd known: not really a start, but they moved their heads at the unexpected sound.

She stood up and answered the door. "Chandra!" she said when she saw the foppish Indian standing there.

"Delilah," he answered. "I must speak with you."

There was a tight knot in Tsali's stomach, a sharp pain, one he'd never felt before. Something about the way the two of them spoke to each other and looked at each other told him loudly and clearly that they'd . . . that they'd done *that* with each other.

But this was Beeker's woman! This was the woman who he himself dreamed of coming to live with them!

Tsali was undone. How could Billy Leaps live with this? he wondered. How horrible it must feel to know that the woman you loved was doing those things with other men, unworthy other men like Chandra!

How could he ever look at her the same way?

She brought Chandra into their suite, and they sat down. Somehow, through his shock and his hurt, Tsali told himself that he had to follow their conversation.

"I have new information. I don't understand it all. That's why I had to take the chance of coming here."

"Of course," Delilah answered.

"The bombs—the nuclear bombs. How are they set off?"

"There are many ways, Chandra. What do you mean?"

"Can it be done with simple dynamite?"

"Yes. That can be used to set off the explosion."

"They don't have to be dropped from the air, then?"

"No, not at all."

He sighed and went on. "I overheard my brothers giving

instructions to two teams of men who've been training near Agra. They're some of the most fanatical of the troops.

"They're being sent, one team to Bombay, the other to Calcutta. They were told that they were to have the great honor of destroying Islamic strongholds in each city. On the surface, that task would make sense—at least to them. But I knew it was impossible that it was so simple.

"They were also told that they should drive large trucks up to the buildings. They were told that the trucks contained dynamite. But I know that the explosive charges alone couldn't take up the whole of a truck bed.

"This must be the way they're going to set off the nuclear explosions."

"The bombs could easily fit in a truck," Delilah said. "There's no question about that. They're sending those men on a suicide mission."

"They wouldn't hesitate to do that."

Tsali heard all of it, but it didn't take away from the shock of his insight. He couldn't stand to look at Delilah for another minute. He moved away from them and turned on the television.

The picture flickered on. There was Patchel at yet another of his huge rallies. The camera moved in for a close-up. Tsali was relieved that he didn't have to watch the rest of their conversation. With his back to them, he couldn't read their lips or see their intimacy, which he was quickly growing to hate.

Then he felt Chandra's hand on his shoulder pushing him aside. He nearly hit the Indian man, surprised that he actually liked having a reason to hit him. He also liked knowing that, with the training he'd received from the men, he was able to strike a good blow. But the expression on Chandra's face stopped him.

"That's not my father!" Chandra was clearly puzzled.

"What do you mean?" Delilah moved closer to the television.

"That's not him! He's a fake. I—it would fool anyone else. It's a remarkable likeness. But it's not my father."

The face on the screen showed its own surprise just then. The camera moved away from the close-up and aimed upward into the sky. A helicopter seemed to be moving toward the Bombay coliseum. The guards behind the man on stage were shown next. They were aiming their machine guns at something above them, it appeared.

The camera zoomed back in to catch the face of the man who was supposed to be Patchel. He was looking straight up in the air by then. Someone had a hand on his shoulder, as if trying to pull the fake Khalifa from the podium.

The camera jerked around; then the helicopter filled the screen. But something else was going on. The Lynx wasn't moving. Then it lifted up, away from the stadium. The camera moved wildly. It panned the arena; it was obvious that the crowd was panicking. The camera showed the stage again, and the man who was supposed to be Patchel was sprawled on the floor. The focus cleared up, and the camera moved in for an intimate shot.

Tsali knew instantly what had happened. There was a small red spot in the middle of the man's head. It was a bullet hole. The "Khalifa" had been assassinated—but not by the helicopter. They'd watched it approach and then leave without firing its weapons.

Tsali turned to Delilah, forgetting her transgression in this moment of confusion. He hoped she'd be able to answer the question.

"Rosie," she said.

"But it was not my father!" Chandra repeated.

"Then we're in even worse trouble than we were before," Delilah answered.

Tsali left them alone. He had to. He couldn't take the chance that they'd want to be alone and go into one of the other rooms of the suite while he was still there. Knowing that Delilah had been unfaithful to his father was bad enough, but to have to actually witness it would have been too much.

He wandered the streets of Delhi, taking in the smells and sights of the capital at night. He couldn't shake off the image of those two together. The assassination receded into the background of his mind, leaving the foreground to this other, more desperate situation.

He couldn't filter out the different feelings he had about it all. He was ashamed that part of him wanted to think less of Beeker because of this. But how could he think his father anything less than perfect after all that'd gone on between them? But another part of him rebelled just as much at the concept of Delilah as a bad woman. She couldn't be. She'd given Billy Leaps so much pleasure. A man that good couldn't fall in love with a bad woman; Tsali couldn't imagine that. He just couldn't.

He finally gave up his wandering and made his way back to the hotel. Maybe they'd have done *it* by now and he could make believe that it hadn't really happened. That would be how he'd handle it. He'd keep it a secret for the rest of his life.

He was close to the hotel. He turned the last corner, then reflexively shrunk backward, his spine against the wall of the building.

At first he thought they were going away together. If that was the case, he didn't want them to see him. The other men with them must be servants, a chauffeur and maybe a bodyguard. But then he saw that the bulge in one of the men's suit pockets was actually a gun barrel aimed at them.

Delilah and Chandra weren't being helped into the back of the enormous Rolls-Royce limousine; they were being pushed. They were being taken captive.

Tsali responded immediately to the danger, taking in the variables. Then he realized what a fool he'd been. He'd forgotten everything his father had taught him—he'd left the hotel unarmed. He didn't have his pistol with him, the arm he was supposed to carry at all times.

If he'd had the Colt, he might have been able to act. But as it was, he couldn't do a thing. He was just a disabled teenager on the streets of Delhi, as naked as he could be, as unable to defend his father's woman as an inept bureaucrat.

This, he swore to himself, was a mistake he would never make again. He fought back the urge to wallow in self-deprecation. This wasn't the time for it. This was the time to remember the rest of his lessons. He should go to the Black Berets now. He should take them the intelligence he'd gathered and be there with them when they acted.

He felt his back pants pocket. His wallet was there, and inside were the plastic credit cards that Beeker hated but that Cowboy had demanded they all use for their expenses so he could keep track of them.

He was going to use them, he knew as he watched the Rolls pull away from the hotel. He didn't dare go back inside. He didn't want to gamble that there were other men waiting for him.

He'd take the credit cards and fly to Bombay tonight. Harry was there; he'd be able to reach Harry through Mr. Batliwalla. And he assumed that Rosie and Cowboy were there as well. He needed them. He needed to make sure they had all the news he did. And he needed them to recapture his father's woman. No matter what she'd done, she had to be saved.

He'd deal with the rest of it later. Maybe.

15

Tsali paid the taxi driver in Bombay an exorbitant amount of money to drive him to Mr. Batliwalla's house. None of the cabbies had wanted to go into the city. Too much rioting, they'd complained. The one who'd seen the number of bills that the strange-looking boy offered finally agreed.

As they drove, Tsali could see signs of destruction all around. Shells of burned-out cars lined the streets. There were military patrols all over, their bayonets poised and, he knew, their rifles loaded.

The driver dropped him at Batliwalla's house. The Cherokee boy went up and pounded his fist on the door. Someone looked out through the peephole and then opened the door.

It was Batliwalla's servant, the same one who'd come upon them on the street when he and Harry had been attacked. He grabbed Tsali and dragged him inside as quickly as he could, then slammed the door shut again. He did a little bow and waved him into the house.

Harry was there, drinking tea with Mr. Batliwalla. The Greek looked at him with an expression of surprise. "What's up, Tsali?"

The boy's hands talked for him. *Delilah's in trouble. Someone took her away in Delhi. And the man who was shot wasn't Patchel.*

"Are you sure?" Harry stood up. "But the whole place is going bonkers over the shooting! There's been violence between the Din Illahi followers and members of the other religious groups. They're blaming them for the assassination of their emperor."

It wasn't him. His own son said so.

"Rosie had a fallback, kid. I think it's time to activate it—right now!"

"What are you talking about? Where are you going?" Mr. Batliwalla was shocked at how this supposedly levelheaded Greek merchant was acting. He'd only understood the spoken part of the conversation; he didn't follow Tsali's sign language.

"Forget it, Batliwalla. I have things to do."

"The gold exchange!"

"Later, Batliwalla. Much later."

Then Harry was leading the way out of the building. He stopped just inside the front door and pulled out his Colt. He nodded to Tsali; it was just between them. Then he put it back in its hidden holster. They had that pistol between them, at least. They were armed.

But Tsali hadn't even been worried about that. As soon as he was with one of the Black Berets, he felt fine. He knew they'd handle the situation—once they were together.

Rosie was sitting at the bar of a modern hotel near the beach in Bombay. He was staring at his double Scotch. He'd been there for hours. He'd had two of the drinks; that was all. He'd wanted more, but something was stopping him from getting drunk.

What?

There was no damned answer that was any good. He wanted to have some booze. He'd just killed a man—that was one of the best reasons for a stiff drink he knew. But something kept him from doing it.

He didn't want to go outside the hotel. The riots were wreaking havoc all over the city. The religious hatred of the Din Illahi was being vented on everyone they could find.

It wasn't all that dangerous for him to be there. It would take days for the Bombay police to figure out that this hotel was the source of the death bullet—if they ever did. He'd used a high-powered M16 with a special telescopic lens.

It was one of the new laser jobs. On the battlefield, those could be your own death; the enemy could find you by tracing your visible laser beam back to its source. But the M16 had been perfect in the well-lighted stadium. From his room on a high floor, carefully chosen just for that purpose, Rosie'd been able to aim the gun perfectly. He hadn't fired until the slight green of the laser had appeared on the forehead of the Khalifa.

He'd done what he'd set out to do. But it bothered him that he couldn't have a damned drink to celebrate it or to get over it or to do whatever else men did afterward. But there was something—and it sounded like Beeker's voice.

So he hadn't done it at just the right time. What difference did it make that he'd jumped the timetable a little bit? His job had been to get the leader of the Din Illahi and take him out. Rosie grabbed hold of the Scotch glass. Wasn't that right? Hadn't he done just what he was supposed to do?

The drink wouldn't come up off the bar. The other guys—he knew that was the real problem. He'd fucked up the timing, and they'd be thrown off. He'd forgotten the team. God damn the fucking team! He'd done his job; they could figure out how to do theirs.

The glass came up off the bar now. It touched his lips. But it wouldn't tip backward and let the Scotch flow into his mouth or down his throat. That voice was inside him, struggling to get out.

We're going back . . .

A chill ran up and down his spine as he remembered the words Beeker had spoken when he found Rosie in the basement of the hospital in Newark.

We're going back . . .

And they were back. They'd been back since that very day. There was no use fighting it, he realized. It was a fact of your life, and you have fucked it up, he told himself. You acted on your own. You forgot the team.

This time he had no answer for the self-accusation. There was none—none that could stand up to scrutiny.

There was still the other plan. He'd told them about it in case there was a mess-up, and this sure as hell counted as one. Would they be there? Should he try to meet them? He had to. He suddenly realized that that was the only hope. They had to regroup. They had to get back together again and get their collective asses out of this damned country.

He slammed the glass of Scotch onto the countertop and stood up. He flipped some bills onto the bar and left.

Marty Appelbaum thought the International Medicinal plant was pretty at night. All those chemical compounds being mixed together gave the place an eerie look; it lit up the horizon with all kinds of otherworldly colors.

The smoke that came up from the tall chimneys was illuminated by some of the lights. It wasn't the usual black or gray discharge from the usual industrial smokestack. There were purples and oranges in it. There were greens that you'd never see in nature.

Now, if Rosie or Beeker were here, they'd go on and on

about that; they'd complain that the emissions were proof of the horror of the place and that nature never produced those colors.

Well, it was artistry of a sort, Marty thought. That was all.

He was sitting in the command post he'd constructed for himself. Delilah had come through with all the materials he'd ordered days ago. He'd taken over a peasant's hut on a small rise a mile or so from the plant and had turned the inside of it into a high-tech paradise. Maybe the stereo speakers for the compact disc player were overdoing it, but that was *their* fault.

They'd left him alone out here in the middle of nowhere to watch over an industrial plant while they were having fun. Damn them! They were always cutting him out of the really good action, leaving him to do something faggy like stand guard or figure out how a bunch of amateurs would fuck up a simple explosion.

There was a sudden, loud *beep beep beep* in the house—one of his impromptu warning devices. It was simple, really; he'd figured that anyone trying to blow up a chemical factory wouldn't come in through one of the main highways. They'd be lazy, too, he'd snorted, so they wouldn't have come overland, the way he probably would have. They wouldn't have crossed this peasant's fields, for instance, which would have been perfect. Instead, they'd take a side road into the complex.

So he'd set up a series of light-activated sensors. An infrared beam, invisible to the human eye, was shot across the paths of possible intruders. Whenever one of the beams was broken by a passing vehicle or even a human body, the break would set off the alarm.

Marty went out the door, noting which alarm had sounded, and looked out over the plain.

Oh, no!

What a stupid plan! A bunch of goddamned bozos! Couldn't the guys at least have given him a decent set of adversaries?

He'd sat there for days and wondered what was the most ridiculously easy and obvious way to blow up the complex.

SA-7s were the answer. He'd figured that out after hearing Cowboy describe smuggling them into Afghanistan and how easily the kids had used them. Now, Marty would have wanted something much more delicate. He wouldn't have wanted evidence of even a quasi-military action, for one thing. But more important, he thought as he gazed again at the pretty colors coming from the smokestack, he'd have wanted something aesthetically pleasing. If you're going to take out something that looked as nice as this chemical complex, at least do it with style!

But two truckloads of idiots were now driving right up the most obvious of the side roads. They were real turkeys, he decided. They weren't cool the way Beeker was when he wanted to look nonchalant about something. Or Rosie! Hell, the big black guy could make you forget he could tear you apart with his own hands, he could look so cool sometimes.

Marty forgot about the attackers approaching the chemical plant for a moment and tried to mimic Rosie's best walk, the one that could end up with a high-five to a buddy. He scowled. He knew he couldn't carry it off. He'd have to ask the guy to teach him. But Rosie hated it when Marty asked for things like that.

Then Marty realized that Rosie would *really* hate it if those assholes got any closer to the plant.

He went back inside the house and sat down at his controls. The panel looked like the cockpit of the Space Shuttle. It was covered with small lights and little knobs and switches. He'd had so much free time, he'd really worked on it. He turned a switch to lower the volume of the heavy-metal music blaring in his ears. Then he turned another. That activated something—anyone could tell, because a series of lights came on. Marty looked out the window in front of him and gauged the location of the trucks. Just one more second here . . .

Then he turned the first knob.

The kaboom of the explosion sent the vehicle flying whole into the sky. It sent down little stick figures that Marty figured were human beings—or at least that had been human beings.

The second truck stopped short when its driver understood what had happened. It was backing up now. Marty had considered that possibility in his planning. He smiled at the predictability of these jokers.

He put his hand on another switch; the sounds of the heavy-metal group were just picking up then. "Perfect!" he yelled in appreciation to the driver, who couldn't possibly understand him. "Just perfect!" He knew this piece of music by heart. Now, if the driver would wait just one more second . . .

Marty's finger was poised, waiting for the riff to build to its crescendo. Then . . . "*Yes!*" The switch was pulled, and the second *kaboom* sounded, in perfect time with the music.

Oh, was that pretty!

Marty got up and danced around the dirt floor of the hut. "Oh, that was just about the best I've ever done!" He moved to the knob to turn up the music for the next cut of the album. He deserved to celebrate! Yes, indeed, let those other assholes desert him. He could still have a great time!

Marty went into high peak, ready for anything. He shouldn't have celebrated so quickly. The music suddenly was turned off. Damn it, if Harry had been there, he wouldn't have done this, and he would have heard the new warning. If Harry hadn't left him alone . . .

But then Marty dropped his hands, which had been in a perfect martial arts position.

Harry *was* there. Right there. He was holding the wires that connected the compact disc player to its speakers.

"Marty, how the hell did you know that's how they would try and get in there?" Rosie asked. The big black man was standing between Tsali and Harry.

"Well," Appelbaum said sheepishly, "Harry said to figure out how someone who wasn't as good as I was would do it, and be prepared."

Rosie looked around at the museum of high-tech equipment that had been amassed in the primitive hut. Over in one corner—its presence answered an unspoken question—was a gasoline generator that produced enough electricity to power all this crap.

"But what if they'd come in a different way?"

"Well"—Marty blushed—"I had other plans."

He moved to his console. He'd spent all his waking hours at this. Now he knew it was worth it. "I figured out the options, see? I figured out every possible way they could have approached the place."

Then Marty began turning the knobs and pulling the switches. He knew it was as beautiful as the music he'd just been listening to. He knew he'd created a special work of art, his unique contribution.

The other three were drawn to the door as the sounds began. They were louder, more insistent, and more compelling than what'd come from the speakers earlier.

They watched in amazement as a rainbow of artificial colors lit up the skies around the chemical plant. Torrents of blue, showers of orange, fountains of deadly red—all of them were accompanied by blasts of noise.

Kaboom!

Bab-bab-BAM!

One after another, after the slight hesitation that you get in a fireworks show when you're not right by the missiles, the sounds struck their ears to play a discordant multimedia spectacular.

But this couldn't really be compared to a sideshow on the Fourth of July. This was much more. As they stood in awe, they watched the might of modern technology exploding in front of them. This was a vision of the final conflict. The ground shook under their feet. The illumination from the confabulation was bright enough to hurt their eyes.

They imagined the one great battle in history. They had to think of the destruction of the human race. In that one moment they were viewing more raw power and energy than they'd ever dreamed existed. And it was all under the control of one man. Marty Appelbaum was orchestrating the dress rehearsal for the end of the world.

Then just as suddenly, punctuated by only a few lingering flamelike lights, it was over. The entire show had lasted seconds. There were only gentle sounds now: of earth falling back to the earth, of man-made winds moving through the air.

"And see!" Marty said. "I didn't do a damned thing to that fucking complex. You told me to leave it alone, and I did. I put bombs that could blow up an *insect* that approached the damned place, from any direction. But I figured out how to do it without messing up the plant."

Rosie turned to Marty. He stared at him, speechless at yet another unreal display of his craft.

"Well, don't get mad at me for wasting the stuff, either! Hell, you wouldn't've wanted to carry it out of here, anyway. It took me days to do it, you know? The whole time you guys left me alone, I didn't have anything else to do."

They just kept staring at him.

16

Beeker was finishing up his laps in the Patchel pool. He loathed this more every day, being in a woman's house, being at a woman's beck and call, being a kept boy. Even the pleasure in this exercise was dwindling. This kind of servitude that came from domestication was the reason he'd left his two wives.

He was punishing the water. He was flogging it with all his might. Another time, he might have been aware of his speed and proud of it. That didn't matter now. What mattered was getting the hell out of Agra. He was beginning to lose it. He'd had to will himself to stay here at his post. Now he just wanted out. He didn't know how much longer he could take it.

Finally he had driven himself as close to the point of exhaustion as he could. He swam slowly toward the ladder out of the pool. But as soon as he put his foot on the first rung, he knew he was surrounded.

He looked up and saw Jamshed. On either side of him were three machine-gun-wielding soldiers wearing the supposedly secret uniforms of the army of the Din Illahi.

"My father wants to see you." One of the soldiers looked

at the elder Patchel brother. There was a moment of tension between them. Jamshed rephrased the order: "The Khalifa demands your presence."

The troops were trained—not well, but well enough that Beeker knew one of them would get him with his Karlsrupa before he could act. He was stripped down to swimming briefs. He had nothing to fight with. *It fits*, he told himself with disgust. *This is the way an animal goes to slaughter. All I've been is a dancing dog for the bitch's pleasure.*

He finished his climb up out of the pool. As soon as he was there, two of the men jumped on him and attached metal restraints to his wrists behind his back.

He was still dripping water with his arms clasped behind him when they dragged him to Patchel. The man had definitely gone over the edge. The old, formal furnishings in the living room were gone. In their place were a dais and throne for the Khalifa and another, slightly lower, for Nur.

The two elder sons were the only members of the audience. Now Beeker understood why the soldier had dared to confront Jamshed at the pool. He'd known that the man wasn't one of the real rulers. He would have been more reticent if it'd been Nur out there.

Beeker refused to act with anything that approached subservience. He stared at Nur with open loathing. He glared at her father with disdain.

"Such a shame," Nur said with a dangerous purr to her voice. "You had such potential in the bedroom."

Papa Patchel wasn't going to enter into the joking. He clapped his hands. There were scuffling noises behind Beeker. He turned to see what they could be.

Delilah!

His mind reeled at the sight of the woman. She'd been

beaten. One eye was swollen shut. Her blouse had been ripped open, and one of her breasts was exposed. It was covered with deep purple bruises.

Beside her was Chandra. He was in even worse shape. His shirt had been totally torn off, and there was blood crusted on his skin.

The two of them looked despondent, defeated. He knew what caused that look. No human being—not even a Black Beret—can withstand expertly applied torture. Anyone, man or woman, will break in the hands of someone who knows that despicable trade. But it didn't help someone who'd given in to recognize that. They still had feelings of having betrayed a trust, of having committed a sin of unspeakable weakness.

They had told everything. That was why Beeker was here in shackles. The operation was over.

"Your foolish men have handed me the perfect opportunity. It's one I'd actually counted on. I was obviously not in the amphitheater in Bombay. That was an actor especially made up to look like me," Patchel was saying. "But all India saw me murdered.

"Tomorrow, here in Agra, they will witness my resurrection. Any doubters will be converted. From my funeral bier, I will rise, reborn—the true god and emperor of India.

"On my command the contaminated cities of Bombay and Calcutta will be destroyed by a nuclear bolt from heaven.

"The government in Delhi will disintegrate. The masses of India will rise up and praise me, willing to be ruled by me. When I choose to leave this mortal world, my heir will reign in my place." He put a hand on Nur and smiled at his beloved daughter.

"The dynasty will be established for all time.

"Tonight I will announce my intentions to my inner circle.

I will explain to those who must understand just what is to happen. To prove to them that I am committed to this, I have reinstituted the *hom*. To give them proof of my belief in the need to cleanse India, I will offer to the *hom* as the first sacrifice my own son—the one contamination of my family." He stared down at Chandra. "And he will go to his fiery sacrifice with the foreign infidels by his side.

"Take them away. Prepare them for tonight!"

Men grabbed Beeker's arms. Others took hold of Delilah and Chandra. As they were being dragged away, he could hear Nur shouting, "Long life to the Khalifa!" He swore she called it out as passionately as she'd called out his name during sex.

Night was falling on the Hindustan plains. They'd hardly had any sleep in the past twenty-four hours. It didn't matter. They were ready. They were at peak. They were prepared.

"We're doing this right."

Roosevelt Boone stood in the middle of the small group of men and looked each one of them in the eyes. There was something menacing about the man. There was an expression on his face that they hadn't seen in weeks, even months. It was something like what they might have seen on Patchel's face. It had something to do with madness.

"We're doing this like the Black Berets."

Boone began to undress. No; you couldn't say he simply *took* off his clothes. He was *tearing* them off. Each time he ripped off a garment, he removed something from himself that had to go. They all followed his example.

Not one of them said a word. They stripped down to their skins. Then each reached down and took clothing from the pile on the ground.

Cowboy was the first to step into the olive drab underclothing.

White wouldn't have done. Even a sliver of white shorts showing would have been a target for an enemy.

The feel of the cotton shouldn't have been different from any other he'd put on. But it was. It was different. It was the start of the uniform.

Who but a Marine like Billy Leaps Beeker could've understood how important that was to a man? Who but a Marine could have explained what it did to someone when he shed his other clothing and joined his compatriots in donning a uniform?

Cowboy felt his skin tighten. These past few days had been . . . Something wracked his body inside. It was like a sob, but more like a shudder. No one paid any attention to it. Everyone in his own way was experiencing the same thing.

Harry stepped into the camouflage pants. They were tight enough that no spare fabric would be a catch on them, but they were loose enough that there was no movement that a man might have to make that he couldn't. He cinched the belt; the buckle had been carefully tarnished with a mixture of steel wool and gasoline so that it wouldn't shine. Even the dimmest moonlight bouncing off a small piece of steel like this could have spelled death.

He sat down on the damp ground and pulled on the dark socks and the jungle boots. He stood back up and retrieved one of the shirts; it was of the same camouflage material of varying dark shades of olive and brown, black and green. He was buttoning it up when he looked over and saw Tsali dressing as seriously as the rest of them.

A boy. Just a teenager. Just a kid. He shouldn't know about this stuff, not at his age. Harry stopped what he was doing and studied Tsali for a minute.

If we get out of this alive, I'm going to . . .

But he couldn't finish the thought. He didn't have a clue

what you did with a seventeen-year-old boy nowadays. And he realized that if he ever did find out, it wouldn't be something you did with Tsali. Not after the life he'd led with them. Not after the life they'd all led.

Rosie wasn't having those thoughts. He was the leader this time. It was his show for this round. Their entire operation had fallen apart. He may have been one of the reasons for that, but he wasn't going to worry about it now. Leaders don't deal with hindsight. Leaders deal with the resources they have on hand in the present and the opposition they face today. They don't rest on past laurels, and they don't mourn yesterday's defeats.

He looked around at the men. There were only five of them, and one of them was the adolescent Tsali. But he was needed. They were all needed. They all knew that.

Rosie was the first to finish dressing. He had another ritual to perform, his own very personal one. He picked up a straight-edge razor. They all watched him now. This happened every time the team went into battle.

Rosie carried the blade over to Tsali. The boy stared at the sharp metal, the only thing left among them that caught the receding light of the evening.

Then Rosie knelt in front of the teenager. Tsali carefully put the blade down and then took some water from a canteen. He used it to lather up a bar of soap. He smeared the suds over Rosie's head.

Why did the huge black man have his skull shaved every time? They never knew. They'd never gotten an answer. But he wouldn't enter battle without doing it. From one of his ears hung an earring, a skull. The small white oval was a shocking contrast to his richly dark chocolate flesh. After he was shaved, Rosie took on the aura of that skull. It wasn't something you could see. It was something you *sensed about* him. After he'd gone through his ritual, Rosie had no fear of anyone who claimed supernatural powers.

Perhaps that's why they were so awed by his personal institution. They had an idea, one that rational Westerners would never take seriously, that Rosie moved into the arena of the dead at these times.

They couldn't think of that. They couldn't give credence to the thought. But they couldn't deny that every time they watched him do this, they remembered him standing in the lower reaches of the hospital in Newark, pulling the skin off the dead bodies of accident victims, singing them lullabies as sweet as a mother's, serenading them with the warmth of a special loved one.

Tsali took the blade now and made long strokes on Rosie's head. Every move he made took off white lather and left the dark brown of his skin. The boy was careful, as careful as he could be. And he was reverent, as serious as he knew how to be, just the way any of the rest of them would be if they were doing this now.

When it was over, there were tears in Cowboy's eyes. Harry couldn't look at the rest of them. Marty was silent and somber. Tsali stood with his mouth agape. Rosie stood up in front of him, his mouth frozen in a wide smile.

Rosie reached into his pocket and pulled out a tin of cammy grease. He opened it and stuck his fingers into the ooze. He brought their tips up to Tsali's face and began to paint. He started with sweeping strokes on the boy's cheeks, then across his forehead. He finished with dabs on his nose, chin, and throat.

He was painting him, applying the war paint of the ancient Cherokee warriors, transforming him as surely as the shave had transformed himself. Then when he was finished, he handed the can to Tsali. This was part of it, too. You reciprocated, as if just as no man should have to be the only one applying the grease, no man should have to live without having it done to him, either.

Tsali saw all around that the rest of the men were doing the same thing.

This was a gentle ritual. It always seemed strange to see such large, powerful men touching each other's faces so easily, to see their strokes of painting received so trustingly.

When they were all finished, when Rosie's hands had finished their caress and left their marks over his face, Tsali looked around again. He realized he'd lost himself in the group. He wasn't alone; he wasn't isolated. He was part of them. This, he knew, was the right way. This was the way the Black Berets did it.

"Now," Rosie said, "we're ready."

17

Beeker looked out over the crowd of onlookers. All the expected types were there; he recognized them all. There were crazed true believers whose vacant eyes betrayed their fanaticism. There were the calculating gazes of hangers-on, ones who thought they were going with the winner. And there were ones whose political views he'd never know. They were packed into the courtyard of the Patchel mansion to see the public spectacle of death.

They were the kind who'd packed the Coliseum in Rome to watch the gladiators die, who had screamed for wrestlers to murder one another in the ring, who weren't satisfied if a single hockey player left the rink without shedding blood.

Delilah, Chandra, and Beeker stood naked in bondage on a platform, prepared for the *hom*. He could only register that this wasn't what he'd expected. He'd thought it'd be like a witchcraft trial. He'd pictured them tied to a stake, tinder and logs at their feet, flames growing up at them.

Instead, they were standing over intensely hot coals. There seemed to be a sea of them only a few feet below them. They were going to be thrown onto the embers. He quickly calculated

143

the heat of the fire. The embers were something like charcoal; the fire was so hot, it'd already consumed the material that produced the flames. It was a glowing, living mass of red and orange.

A piece of paper was caught by the wind and sent aloft into the air. It approached the embers. Even before it could land the paper was consumed by the heat. It exploded into combustion. That was what would happen to them.

At least, he realized, it would be quick.

Patchel was in his most extravagant robe. Nur sat beside him. The father was studying the crowd, taking its measure, wanting the timing of this evening's activities to be perfect. But Nur was watching Beeker. The same lust was in her expression that he'd seen when they'd been alone. She liked this, the vulnerable and bound lover. She'd remember this for years after he'd died—he was sure of it.

What a lousy way to go! He was disgusted with himself and with the lot of them. There was—there had always been—in his mind the image of a warrior's death for himself. He'd grown up nurturing the memory of his father, a brave Cherokee who'd gone to Korea in the Marine Corps and had died in battle. That was nobility.

But this wouldn't be that kind of death. This wouldn't be a quick release in the throes of war. This was a slaughter of warriors who'd forgotten their calling.

He looked over at Delilah. Right now there was nothing sexual to him about her nudity. He saw only her vulnerability and the visual evidence that he'd failed her. For him to die this way was bad enough. For his woman to was the height of humiliation and disgrace.

What gods were there? He'd wondered about that—not often, but enough. He'd dreamed as a boy and even recently about a place where the Cherokee went to the final rest. In his vision and in the stories of the old people, it was a place of honor. But if it existed, he couldn't travel there. A man who died like this couldn't pass its gates.

The music in the background was picking up. Patchel stood up, as if on cue. The crowds moved toward him; his motions distracted them from the entertainment—the condemned awaiting their fate.

The chants of the Din Illahi filled the night air. The faithful were being called to worship. The emperor was beginning the convocation. The *hom* would soon be honored.

Billy Leaps Beeker prepared to die.

Cowboy flew the Lynx 3 through a pass and over the supposed factories. There were lights all over the place. Crowds of men were running around in and out of the fake industrial buildings.

The soldiers of the Din Illahi were on the move. He'd arrived just in time.

None of them paid attention to the armored helicopter. They ignored it, obviously thinking it was one of their own. As yet untested in battle with an armed enemy, they hadn't learned the vital necessity of being able to identify your foe's weapons. A trained soldier would have known that this wasn't one of his own forces' Messerschmitts.

That was too bad, Cowboy thought as he turned the Lynx back toward the main building. That was really too bad.

He would begin with the TOWs. His fingers touched the controls and prepared to fire the deadly rockets. He remembered that he had come close to wasting the weapons of one of these copters when he had almost fired them just to kill one man, Patchel. Would his stupidity have meant Beeker's death? Probably.

It made him all the more intent on making sure that these missiles found their target perfectly. He stopped the copter in midair and tilted it toward the roof of the huge plant. Only then, at the sight of that strange maneuver, did some of the soldiers on the ground look up at him.

Just as they did, they saw four of the powerful missiles ignite and begin their screaming journey through the air toward their target.

There were four almost-simultaneous explosions as the missiles tore through the top of the building and landed on target. The missiles had been aimed perfectly. Too perfectly; their impact was too clustered. There were secondary explosions when a couple of the hidden Messerschmitts' fuel tanks went up. But that wasn't enough to wipe out the arsenal.

There were only the grenades now. Cowboy moved in closer. Some of the Din Illahi were reacting. There were small *pings* as bullets glanced off the skids of the Lynx. If one of the men got lucky and hit his fuel tanks or the vital machinery of the rotor, he'd be gone.

But you don't worry about that in the middle of a battle. You don't consider your mortality. You only think of the objective. At least, that was the way you went about it while wearing the uniform of the Black Berets.

The grenades had much smaller payloads than the TOWs. He had to be much more careful about their placement. He got the copter moving. The Lynx was making a run; its sudden speed threw off the gunmen, although that wasn't his real purpose. His real purpose was to have the bird drop its presents on the building at precise intervals. If he could get just the right fuel tanks to blow up close enough to the others, the Messerschmitts would never make it out of the makeshift hanger.

The Lynx dropped its deadly grenades just the way he wanted them to. The small explosions sounded behind him as he sped along the length of the building. Then just as he'd planned, there were louder detonations as the fuel in the Messerschmitts went.

He pulled up sharply at the end of the run. The building was being consumed by the conflagration. No soldiers fired at him. They were running instead, running for their lives. Some of them had flames shooting up from their own uniforms.

There'd be death in the camps of the Din Illahi tonight. There'd be mourning in the homes of Agra. Cowboy felt sorry for all the people involved; he truly did. But he couldn't help it if they'd chosen to be on the side opposite the Black Berets.

It wasn't his fault that they'd made the worst mistake of their lives.

The sounds of the explosions carried to the Patchel mansion. Father and daughter turned, stunned, and saw the flames rocketing up into the air. The first noises had been small, when Cowboy had sent the TOWs to their target. Then the explosions had increased in intensity when his grenades had found their mark. But now, as the ammunition that had stupidly been stored in close quarters was being eaten by the flames in the warehouse, the detonations were as powerful as any that Papa Patchel had himself planned for the morning.

The crowd shrank back from the glowing embers that awaited the *hom*. They weren't looking in awe at the new dynastic leaders anymore. They were worried. Concern spread among them. Had they chosen the wrong people?

Rosie knew the answer.

Cowboy's attack had been right on schedule. The synchronicity that had saved the Black Berets time and time again was back. He didn't have to worry about the other men; this time he knew they were at their stations. This time he knew he could count on them, just the way they could count on him.

He moved quickly to take out the solitary guard at the sector of the wall protecting the Patchel mansion. He'd taken strong wire and two pieces of wood and constructed a makeshift garrote. The result wasn't pretty, but it was damned effective.

Rosie threw the wire over the back of the man's head. When he pulled it back, it caught on the front of the guard's throat. The poor bastard didn't even have time to register the attack. Rosie jerked the garrote toward himself. The wire cut through the vulnerable flesh of the throat, stopping only when it reached the man's neckbone. When Rosie threw the man and the primitive weapon down onto the ground, the head rolled backward, like a broken doll's head barely attached to the rest of his body. And it had no more life in it than a doll's head, either.

It didn't matter. He'd been dead from the second Rosie had begun.

Rosie took the assault rope from around his chest and unraveled it. The hook on one end acted as a weight to increase its velocity with added centrifugal force; he sent the thing flying through the air. The hook caught on the top of the high wall the first time. Rosie'd known it would. He'd never doubted it.

He tugged to make sure it was secure. Then, using the rope for purchase, he walked up the sheer side of the wall. There was a passageway at the top, the kind that medieval castles used to have as a last line of defense. There soldiers might be walking patrol now. One of them might have seen the hook. He might be waiting for Rosie at the top. It might be the end.

But you never think about that in the middle of a battle. You don't worry about it. You just do your job. If you don't make it through, then maybe one of the others can achieve the objective.

That was what mattered now: the objective. Not personal glory; not even self-preservation. Not when you'd put on the uniform of the Black Berets.

Rosie got to the summit and stood. His M16 swept around him. There was a corpse a few feet away; its neck was as cleanly severed as the one Rosie'd cut down on the ground. Standing over it was Tsali. The kid didn't seem to register any emotion. He'd left that stuff behind, the stuff of regular people. He wasn't even angry or hurt as he witnessed what was going on down below.

Rosie turned and saw Beeker and the other two standing on the platform over the coals. *Don't worry, Beak, old pal. This isn't the day you meet your maker. This is the night you walk out of here with good friend Rosie.*

He took in the forms of the other camouflaged, uniformed men who'd assumed strategic parts of the wall overlooking the courtyard.

They were waiting for him. He smiled when he saw Papa Patchel on his throne. He took his aim carefully this time. There was no need for anything fancy like lasers. He didn't need that.

He pictured Patchel just the way he had in his dreams— between the cross hairs of his sight. His finger began to squeeze the trigger. Then came the beautiful, familiar, loving sound of a bullet speeding out of a gun barrel toward a target.

Tsali had his own M16 trained. Sweat gathered in his crotch and under his arms. His father and Delilah were there, unable to resist, about to be thrown onto those terrible coals.

Now beads of perspiration were gathering on his forehead as well.

He watched with dread as two of the men from the Din Illahi moved toward the three captives. They took hold of Chandra. They moved him without effort toward the edge of the platform.

He knew he could take them both, if only Rosie would . . .

Then he saw the response of the black man's M16. Instantly,

Tsali pulled the trigger of his own rifle. One of the guards who stood by Chandra fell to his knees and then fell forward onto his face. Before the other could even understand what had happened, another of Tsali's bullets found him. He catapulted over the edge of the platform.

There was a sudden collective movement as the crowd saw the body hit the coals. Even if he couldn't hear them, Tsali knew they were screaming. He could see their mouths fly open in fear.

For an instant nothing seemed to have happened to the man; there was just the fact he'd fallen. But then his clothes evaporated in a cloud of steam. And almost as quickly, his flesh seemed to take on a life of its own. It bubbled up; the skin pulled away from the rest of the body.

Then there was hardly anything left but pure white bone. The body seemed almost to disintegrate into a slight amount of matter. Ashes to ashes, dust to dust.

But none of that registered on Tsali. He simply took it in and went on to the next assignment: to sight and obliterate anything in a Din Illahi uniform. The M16 kept sounding its jerking ballet. All around him the rest of the team fired into the crowd, picking off those who appeared ready either to fight back or to try to make their way to Beeker, Delilah, and Chandra in attempt to finish off the sacrifice.

The whole thing was miraculous. They were back! The Black Berets were together again.

18

Then they were all back home in Louisiana. They were sitting on the ledges of the sauna that'd been built onto their house. Tsali couldn't follow their conversation because the rising steam interfered with his view. He didn't care. He didn't have to know what they were saying to one another.

He closed his eyes and imagined they were in one of the sweat-houses of the old people. There, he'd been told, the Cherokee rid their bodies of imperfections. The sweat carried away the poisons that'd entered their minds and clouded their visions. It was one of the steps toward purification.

The surface of his body was running with sweat now. He could feel a bit of dehydration from it all. It was nearly time to leave. He watched his father stand up and go toward the door. Slowly, one by one, the rest of them followed. Tsali was the last to walk through the portal and into the main building.

The way led directly into the communal shower; there were no private bathrooms in the house. It was actually, in its own way, as much of a mansion as Patchel's had been in India. But this was a mansion for fighting men to live in; Beeker had insisted on that.

Each of the men took one of the showerheads and turned on a stream of water. Just as his father had taught him, Tsali kept his own water as cold as he could tolerate. The difference in temperature between the water and the sauna was exhilarating. He shivered under the chilly flow, and he was embarrassed by the physical response his body had to the cool water, but that wasn't important. No one's manhood was being measured that way here.

He was the first to leave, and he toweled off on the other side of the same room. He carefully avoided looking at the others' bodies as they continued to rinse off. He'd be like them soon, as physically mature and as strong, his muscles bulking out. It would come soon. Now he had no need to hurry anything along.

Tsali walked down the hallway. Off to the side of it they each had a cubicle. These, too, were rooms whose makeup had been determined by Billy Leaps. All a man needed was a cot, a simple desk and chair, and a basic bureau and small closet. That was more than enough. That was more than Tsali had ever had before. He couldn't imagine wanting—and certainly not needing—anything more.

He put aside the towel he'd used to cover himself and stepped into an athletic supporter. Then he pulled on a pair of shorts and a strap T-shirt. He decided against wearing anything on his feet.

The others were only just then coming out of the shower. He could see their lips move as they talked to one another in a friendly manner.

He imagined that Cowboy would be back on track soon. It'd take a while still, but the flier had begun to tentatively talk about other women, especially new Latin favorites he'd met in Shreveport not far from this house. No one was rushing him. No one was pressing the issue. They trusted Cowboy; Tsali certainly did. This was the man who, like an elder brother, had initiated him into the wonders of sex. This same man was in pain now. They simply wouldn't talk about intimate things until that hurt had eased.

They'd worried about the pilot. He'd suffered from something that Tsali didn't understand yet, though he did understand that such knowledge would come to him one day, whether he wanted it to or not. There were some things, he now understood, that a man couldn't control. He shouldn't try. He should let them take their course.

As each went into his own room, Tsali walked into the main room of the house.

He hadn't expected her to be there right then. They'd known she'd be there soon but not the exact time of her arrival. The marks and bruises were gone. But he ignored that. He didn't like to think about the past. He was learning more about how to become a man. A man didn't worry about what had been done.

He walked up to Delilah and bent over—happy that he was now tall enough that he had to do that—and let her kiss him on the cheek.

Coffee? he asked her in sign language.

She nodded. He went to the kitchen and put on a pot for her. The men would want some, too. He made a large amount of it, happy to do something they would appreciate. He didn't go back to her but poured a glass of juice for himself from a pitcher in the refrigerator. He stood and stared out the window.

He spotted a pheasant off in the distance. Since she was here, his father would be with her tonight. He wished he didn't blush at that thought, but he still did. He didn't mind. He knew that Beeker would wake up earlier than she would in the morning and that he could get his father to go out and hunt with him. Perhaps with bow and arrows. They'd gotten new ones recently—some kind of high-tech design that Cowboy had found. They'd seemed expensive, but since Chandra had insisted on their taking some of the Patchel family fortune in gratitude, they were richer than ever. The cost of aerodynamically designed arrows was a minor consideration.

He thought little of India these days, even though it had all happened recently. But then, no one was pressing the subject on him or on the rest of the world.

The death of Patchel meant the death of the Din Illahi, just as Akbar's death four centuries ago had sent the religion into oblivion. The Indian government wasn't interested in the world knowing that its secret arsenal of nuclear weapons had been stolen, if only for a brief time. They'd been happy to see the Black Berets leave Delhi, and there were no charges of any kind stemming from the violent confrontation outside Agra.

Even though he understood that he was acting the way the world wanted him to by forgetting all that had gone on in India, Tsali also knew, somehow, that his memory was operating in strange ways for its own reasons, registering only certain things, choosing not to recall others. He knew the image of Chandra that he conjured up now, for example, was incomplete. He didn't worry about some things about him . . . and Delilah.

He turned and saw that Billy Leaps had come into the room, dressed the same as Tsali himself. His father had obviously had the same thought: They'd take a run together. But now Billy Leaps was sitting beside Delilah, who'd moved so that her body was pressed against the big ex-Marine's.

Tsali turned back to the window. Rosie would come running with him. That would be fine. And he'd hunt pheasant with his father tomorrow morning.

This was turning out to be a good vacation for them all, he thought. This was the way it was supposed to be.